VEGAS BOUND

THE SABELA SERIES BOOK 6

TINA HOGAN GRANT

Edited by Crystal Santoro Editorial Services: https://chrissyseditorialservices.org/

Cover Design by T.E.Black Designs – http://www.teblackdesigns.com

Visit The Author's Website

www.tinahogangrant.com

❀ Created with Vellum

CHAPTER 1

JILL

"I still can't believe he is dead." I snuggled closer to Ricky under the satin sheets of our bed, as I reminisced with him about the horrific scene at our wedding. "I've never seen a dead body before, and I never want to, ever again. It was horrible. I keep seeing the image of the knife sticking out of his chest and all that blood. I just can't shake it." The piercing screams from our guests in the room where Davin had been stabbed still echoed in my head.

Ricky pulled me in and kissed my brow. "Me either." He released a heavy sigh. "It kind of puts a damper on our wedding night." He caressed my shoulder as he spoke. "I never met the guy. But from what I've heard about him, it sounds like Slater did the world a favor."

I nodded and raised my head. "Oh, he sure did. Davin was a real jerk. He was sick. Sabela only dated him for half a year when she told him she wouldn't move to Texas with him. He stalked and threatened her. He was obsessed with her. I feel bad for Claire, though; after all, he was her brother. I wonder if she will speak to her parents again? They were lying to her the whole time, and told her they had disowned Davin, when they were still visiting him at the jail on weekends." I shook my head. "I still can't believe he tried to rape Sabela and three other girls. And I thought I knew him."

Ricky agreed. "Yeah, it sucks for them, too. They lost a son. The sad thing is, they blame themselves, and it wasn't their fault. I wish they could see that."

I looked into Ricky's eyes and patted his chest. "I hope Claire can help relieve some of their guilt. Claire is all they have. It's sad."

We laid in each other's arms for the next few minutes, thinking of the horrific incident. I needed to change the somber mood that was lingering over us. "Okay, enough of this dismal chat."

"Starting tomorrow, we will have an entire week in Las Vegas together, and we can spend the whole time locked up in our room if we choose. It will be a great way to spend our honeymoon."

Ricky laughed. "Don't tempt me. I would have no problem being locked up in a room for a week with you. Hey, before we meet my mom and Tony for breakfast, I want to call Slater and see how he is doing. If they decide to keep him in the hospital longer, we may have to cancel our trip. He said he has enough help for the week, but I just want to make sure."

"Why would they keep him in longer? He seemed like he was doing great last night."

"He had a gunshot wound. Even though it was a flesh wound, there is still a chance it could get infected, which could be serious." Ricky raised his hand to his brow. "Man, I can't believe he stabbed Davin in the chest with the cake knife and killed him."

"Thank god he did. He was a raving lunatic, and like the cops said, who knows what would have happened if he didn't. No one knew he had a gun."

I pulled away from Ricky and rested my head on my pillow. "I never dreamed I would be spending our wedding night talking about a dead guy. In our minds, it was supposed to be the triple wedding of the century."

Davin had been obsessed with Sabela since they first met

three years ago. When they went their separate ways, Sabela thought that was the last she'd seen of him, and she soon met and fell in love with Slater. But Davin wasted no time showing his dark side. He threatened and blackmailed Sabela, and even worse, he tried to rape her. Not only did he try to rape Sabela, but he also raped some girls at the university he went to in Texas. The last we heard, he was serving time in jail. That was, until he showed up at our wedding and tried to force Sabela to go with him. When he threatened to kill her, Slater did what any man would do to protect his wife, and grabbed the first thing he saw to use as a weapon, which was the cake knife. Fearing for Sabela's safety, he plunged the knife into Davin's chest, killing him instantly. To our horror, Davin had a gun hidden in his pocket and took a shot at Slater as he fell to his death. Thank god he only has a flesh wound and will be okay, but I have never been so scared in my life.

After spending hours waiting to see Slater in the hospital, we finally made it home around midnight. It's been some wedding night. Neither one of us felt like making love or celebrating our marriage—all I wanted was to be held in Ricky's arms and be close to him. I'm one of the lucky brides that gets to be home with my husband on our wedding night. Poor Sabela is at the hospital with her new husband, so I have no room to complain.

Claire lost her brother, Davin tonight, but she was adamant about confessing no love was lost. She disowned Davin after the rape charges. But their mom, Abigail, couldn't disown her only son as easily, and betrayed Claire by lying to her about visiting him while he was in jail. It's how he found out about our wedding. Claire doesn't know if she can ever forgive or trust her mother again.

Compared to my friends, my life is not so complicated, and I'm relieved to cut ties with my parents, who embarrassed me two days ago over cocktails. Thank god it didn't happen at the wedding.

"Hey, are you okay? You look deep in thought," Ricky asked, as he leaned in and gave me a light kiss on the lips.

I smiled. "Yeah. I was just thinking about everything that had happened, and it wasn't what I had planned for our wedding."

Ricky sighed. "I'll say." He wrapped me in his arms. "Come here. I want to hold you tight while I fall asleep. Tomorrow we start our life together as husband and wife, and hopefully, we will get to celebrate it in Las Vegas."

CHAPTER 2

I stretched from under the covers. The diamond glistening from my wedding ring caught my eye, and I held my hand in mid-air. "Mrs. Jill Ashton," I said aloud with a huge grin. I liked how it sounded and was thrilled that I no longer carried my parent's name—another symbol of breaking the mold. I buried my face in my pillow to silence the screams of joy I released. It was not a dream; I am Ricky's wife.

I turned and looked at Ricky's side of the bed and saw it was empty. The sound of Ricky's voice coming from downstairs piqued my curiosity, and I sat up to listen. The bedroom door was open, and I pinned my ears to eavesdrop on his conversation.

"Are you sure you are going to be okay, man?" I heard Ricky say. "Jill and I have no problem postponing our trip. Just say the word," he added.

I sat up and grabbed one of Ricky's T-shirts draped over the nearby chair and threw it on. When I reached the bottom of the stairs, it sounded like Ricky was winding down the call. Maggie, our Golden Retriever, sprung from her bed and greeted me with excitement as she leaped and pawed my shirt.

"Hey girl," I said with a huge grin as I bent down and gave her some love with many kisses and hugs.

Ricky continued with his conversation. "Well, I'm glad to hear you are doing much better and going home tomorrow. I'll see you next week as long as they cover you at work," Ricky said.

After he had ended the call, I spoke while still petting Maggie. "Everything okay?"

He turned and smiled and held out his arms. I immediately met his embrace and nuzzled my head against his chest, with Maggie trying to squeeze herself between us.

"Yes, that was Slater, and he is doing great. He told me that everything is under control at work and insisted we go to Vegas and have a good time."

I pulled away and did a twirl. "Yippee. It's honeymoon time, baby. What time are we meeting your mom?"

"In about an hour. Hurry and get dressed," Ricky urged. "I'll grab our suitcases and bring them downstairs. We still need to drop Maggie off at Sadie's and Logan's place."

"I still need to take a shower," I said.

"Well, you better hurry. I already took one."

As usual, we were running late, and Ricky texted his mom to let her know we would be at the restaurant around 8:15. After dropping Maggie off, Ricky drove above the speed limit to get to the restaurant.

"We are going to have to make this a quick breakfast. We can't be late for our flight," Ricky said, as we practically ran through the parking lot towards the restaurant.

We spotted Ricky's mom, Linda, and Tony sitting close together in a corner booth. They were both dressed casually in jeans, and Linda wore a light green T-shirt with her blonde hair tied back in a ponytail. Tony looked comfortable with the sleeves of his denim shirt rolled up to his elbows and a few buttons left unbuttoned.

"Hey, mom, sorry we are late," Ricky said, as we scooched into the seat across from them.

Linda gave us a weak smile. "It's okay. I've not slept a wink. How is Slater doing? Every time I tried to close my eyes, I kept hearing the loud sound of a gunshot and seeing Slater fall to the ground. God, that Davin guy could have killed all of us."

Tony wrapped his arms around Linda. "She's been a mess since it happened."

Ricky reached across the table and took his mom's hand. "Hey, it's okay. We are all fine, mom. Slater is going home tomorrow. I'm sorry I abandoned you at the wedding, but there was so much going on, and we needed to get to the hospital."

Linda wiped a tear. "It's okay. We had to stay and wait to be questioned by the police. I didn't expect you to stay behind after they had spoken to you. I hope they won't charge Slater with anything. My god, he saved all of us from that maniac."

Ricky shook his head. "The cop at the hospital said he doesn't foresee any charges being held against Slater because it was clearly self-defense."

Linda held her chest. "Thank god. Well, besides everything that happened, it was a beautiful wedding. Even better without your father there and that bimbo wife of his."

Ricky chuckled. "Yeah, I have to say I was relieved when he said he wouldn't be able to make it. I love dad, but I'm embarrassed by his wife. She could be my sister, for god's sake." Ricky paused. "Do you think you and Tony will ever get married? You guys have been together a long time."

I saw the love seep into their eyes when they turned, looked at each other, and smiled. I hope Ricky and I will still look at each other that way after years of marriage.

Tony was quick to answer Ricky's question. "I've often asked your mom to marry me, but she is afraid it would change our relationship." He smiled again at Linda. "Which is perfect, by the way.

If she ever decides she wants to get married, I will race her down the altar in a heartbeat."

Tony's words melted my heart. "Aww, that is so sweet," I said, before a waitress came to take our order.

"So, are you going to see Annie before you leave?" Ricky asked his mom before taking a sip of his coffee.

"I was really hoping to meet her. It's a pity she couldn't make it to the wedding," I added.

"Your sister is hard to get a hold of," Linda stated. "I was upset and disappointed with her when she said she couldn't make it to the wedding. She told me she was the only one working and couldn't afford to take any time off work. She explained that she makes most of her money in tips. I suggested we go visit her after the wedding, but she said it wasn't a good idea because she is always working." She turned to Tony and smiled. "So we are taking a detour on the way home and spending a few nights at the Grand Canyon."

"Oh, how fun!" I squealed. "I've always wanted to go there."

Ricky was still upset over Annie's boyfriend and shook his head before leaning back in the booth. "What does she see in that loser she is with? Have you ever met him?"

"No, we haven't. I have no idea what he does all day ..." Linda paused. "Do you know we pay for her cellphone? She was about to give it up because she couldn't afford it, and I insisted on paying the bill every month. Otherwise, I'd never be able to talk to her. It's our only form of communication."

Ricky's nostrils flared, and his jaw dropped. "What? You never told me that."

"Well, Annie can't afford to pay for everything on her own."

Ricky's face tightened when he spoke. "When we get back from Vegas, I'm going to drive up to LA and have a talk with that asshole boyfriend of hers. Shit, I don't even have her address. Can you text it to me?"

"Yes, I will, but don't you go causing any trouble," Linda demanded, while pointing a finger.

"Mom, the guy sounds like a sleaze bag and lives off Annie for free. Don't you find it odd that none of us have met the guy?"

"Well, she always sounds happy on the phone and apologetic that she has to work."

"Yeah, I'm not buying it," Ricky said, as he leaned back so the waitress could set down his plate of food.

CHAPTER 3

Ricky remained silent while we ate. I could tell the news about his sister was troubling him, and I sensed his mother knew it too and changed the conversation, directing her questions at me.

"So Jill, do you feel any different now that you are married?"

I giggled and chewed my food before answering. "A little. But we have been living together for a few months, so not much has changed. I guess I feel like I belong now. I didn't like being single. It sucked. You guys really should think about getting married. By looking at you and how you look at each other, I can tell that you are great together."

Linda shook her head. "Oh, no. I don't want to ruffle any feathers. We are fine just the way we are, and being married to Ricky's father was enough."

I shrugged my shoulders. "Okay then."

Ricky wiped his plate clean with a piece of toast, and chugged down the last of his coffee. "Okay, we really gotta go, mom." He turned and gave me a stare. "Are you ready?"

I nodded while taking my last bite of omelet. "Yep, I sure am."

Ricky stood first. "Sorry, mom. I hate to rush off. Call me when you get back home," he said, as he leaned in and kissed his mom on the cheek and then shook Tony's hand. "Come on, Jill, we have to go."

I wiped my mouth with the nearby napkin and smiled at Linda and Tony before standing. "Thank you so much for coming out for the wedding. I just wish the crazy guy hadn't ruined everything."

Linda took my hand. "He didn't. Everything else was beautiful, and you got married, didn't you? I'm thrilled to have you as my daughter-in-law."

I matched her smile. "Thank you so much. That means a lot. Have a great time at the Grand Canyon."

Ricky took my elbow and ushered me out of the restaurant. "Come on, babe. The clock is ticking. Bye, mom. Bye, Tony."

"I'm coming," I replied.

We made it to the airport in the nick of time, with just thirty minutes to spare before our plane began boarding. Once seated on the plane, I leaned into Ricky and gave him a long, sensual kiss on the lips. "I sure do love you."

Ricky chuckled. "Well, I hope so. You married me."

I gave him a loving smile. "I was worried for a while that I would never get married. The thought of spending my life alone scared the crap out of me. Everyone had a boyfriend but me. It was so depressing." I smiled again. "And then you came along. They always say you will meet your forever love when you least expect it." I gave him a big smile and titled my head. "I say it's true. Sabela met Slater when she went to the beach to be alone, and Claire met Travis when her car broke down. And let's not forget Sadie. She met Logan when she was with me in a bar."

Ricky took my hand and leaned back in his seat. "I'm going to have to agree with you. Meeting someone in the waiting room of the hospital where Travis was in a coma was the last thing on my mind." He paused. "Until I saw you."

"Aww, babe. You say the sweetest things." I shifted in my seat.

"So, we have the entire week together in Vegas. What do you want to do?"

Ricky curled his lip and smirked. "If I say it out loud, I may get arrested."

Tuning into his thoughts, I gave his chest a playful slap and whispered in his ear. "Hey, once we're in the air, we could get a head start and do it in the bathroom," I giggled. "Tell me, Ricky, are you a member of the mile-high club? Have you ever done it on a plane?"

Ricky laughed and curled into my body. "Well, now that you mention it, I am not a member." He gave me a devious smile. "Are you?"

I laughed and kissed him again. "I'm not, but I would like to change that." I ran my finger down his chest and let my hand rest between his legs. "Can you help me get my membership?"

"Only if you help me get mine."

I gave his groin a gentle squeeze. "Deal."

CHAPTER 4

*A*fter a restless thirty minutes of sitting on the plane, we finally headed to the runway. I braced myself for my favorite part of flying, the takeoff, which gives me such an adrenaline rush. As the sound of the engines roared and our speed increased, I grabbed Ricky's hand and looked out the window as the plane lifted into the sky. "And we're off," I squealed, as I watched San Diego disappear into the distance. "When do you want to go to the bathroom?" I said with a sultry smile.

Ricky laughed and looked at the signs in the plane's cabin. "The seatbelt lights are still on. Boy, are you in a hurry?"

I looked at the overhead signs and furrowed my brow. "Darn it. I wished they'd hurry up and turn them off."

"Well, when they do, you know everyone is going to race to the bathrooms. Let's wait until the rush is over," Ricky suggested.

I leaned back in my seat and folded my arms. "Fine, but this flight is only an hour, which doesn't leave us much time." I turned and gave Ricky a hard stare. "And I'm not getting off this plane until I am a member of the mile-high club."

He threw me a sexy wink, nudging my shoulder. "Me neither."

A few minutes later, we heard the loud ding of the seatbelt lights being turned off. I grabbed Ricky's hand and shoved him to stand up in the aisle. "Come on, let's go."

Ricky's jaw dropped. "What? I thought we were going to wait."

I pushed him again. "I changed my mind. We will be landing by the time we get into the damn bathrooms. Come on, get up."

Ricky shook his head and laughed as he pulled himself to his feet. "You do realize people will know what we are doing in there, and we can't go in together—one of us has to go in first."

"Good. I don't care if they know. It will be a flight they will remember," I joked. "And I will go in first. I want to make sure it's clean."

Ricky took my hand as we walked single file down the aisle towards the back of the plane, while other passengers were already doing the same. "Hurry," I told Ricky. "If we are one of the first, it's bound to be clean."

"I can't. There are people in front of me," Ricky whispered.

"Damn it," I hissed.

I stomped my feet when I saw all three bathrooms were taken and leaned against the wall with my arms folded.

Ricky tried to ease my frustrations and leaned in, covering his body with mine. Our foreheads touched. "It will be just a few minutes." Suddenly, I heard the click of the door unlock and stood up straight as someone pushed it open. I smiled and kissed Ricky on the lips. "See you in a few minutes."

I quickly closed the bathroom door and scanned the tiny area. "Well, this should be interesting," I mumbled under my breath, as I teased my hair with my fingers and then had a thought. "I'll get a head start." I reached under my shirt, unsnapping my bra, and then pulled it free by reaching up my sleeves. Enjoying the freedom, I gave my boobs a vigorous shake. "Much easier to take off with only one person in here," I said to my reflection in the mirror before stuffing my bra in the corner of the counter. A knock at the door startled me. It had to be Ricky. Who else could it be?

I slid the metal lock with ease and slowly pushed open the door. Ricky wasted no time and quickly entered the bathroom, locking the door behind him. Our bodies pressed tight against each other. "Boy, these are a lot smaller with two people in them," Ricky chuckled.

"I'll say." I breathed in his scent and placed my hands on his chest. "Damn, you smell good."

Ricky was a good six inches taller than me. His height and broad, muscular body were more prominent and noticeable in the tight space where we stood. He towered above me and lowered his head to meet me in a kiss. Embraced by his warm breath and racing tongue, I devoured his mouth and kissed him hard. His chest leaned into mine, pushing me against the wall. There was no room to move or raise my arms, but I didn't care. The kiss was long and sensual and full of passion. I moaned when I felt his hand reach up beneath my shirt and take one of my breasts in his hand. "No bra," he whispered between breaths. "Very sexy."

"And easy access," I whispered back, as I released another moan. He pressed my head against the hard surface of the wall, and then I screamed. "Ouch!"

Ricky jolted back and banged his head in the process against the low ceiling above the sink. "Are you okay? What did I do?"

I tried to move my foot, but I couldn't and winced from the pain. "You are stepping on my foot," I squealed.

Ricky looked down. "Oh, shit." He quickly lifted his foot off mine. He laughed. "This is quite the challenge, and getting into the mile-high club is not that easy."

"Let me lean against the sink. There might be more room from there."

Ricky scanned the tiny bathroom. "No matter where we stand, it's still small."

I slapped his chest. "Very funny, smartass." I squeezed past his magnificent body and cupped my hands around his neck. "Kiss me."

Ricky didn't hesitate. He smiled before smothering me with his lips. My hands now had more room to move, and I reached down and caressed Ricky's prominent bulge. He moaned, and again reached up under my shirt. Still locked in a kiss, he toyed with my breasts. Our passion grew, and our breaths escalated. "Take off your shirt," he whispered.

"How?" I questioned. "I can't raise my arms."

Ricky fumbled with the buttons as I continued to kiss him hard and circle his tongue with mine. After a few minutes, I felt the cool breeze of the air vent above us blanket my skin as Ricky slid my shirt open and pulled it down over my shoulders. He wasted no time, and lowered his head to my chest, circling the nipple with his tongue before taking it in his mouth. "Oh god, yes," I moaned, as I tilted my head back and immediately banged my head on the mirror. "Ouch! Damn it," I yelled.

Ricky immediately stopped and raised his head. "Are you okay?"

I gave a quick nod and directed his head back to my boobs with my hand. "Yes. Don't stop," I told him, as I tried to straighten my body away from the mirror. Ricky's hunger increased as he caressed my breasts and teased me with his warm breath. My moans became louder, and my body craved to be taken by him. His erection was pushing against his jeans as I reached down again. I fumbled with his belt, using only one hand until it came loose, quickly unsnapping the button to his jeans. I smiled at my success and, with haste, slid down his zipper. Ricky moaned and wiggled his hips to give my hand a little room. Now, with some space, I reached down into his jeans and into his underwear, where I finally found his manhood. I took it in my hand and caressed it softly as Ricky's body relaxed and his moans were that of pleasure.

He raised his head away from my breasts and met my lips. The kiss was long and sensual. Our eyes were closed, and our bodies melted as one. "I want you," Ricky whispered.

"Take me," I whispered back, barely leaving his lips.

Ricky grabbed my hips. "Turn around."

"What?"

He held on to my hips and turned my body. "Turn around. It's the only way we can do this."

I giggled at what we were doing as I slowly inched my body around in the tight area until my butt was facing Ricky. I smiled at him through our reflection in the mirror.

"Undo your pants," Ricky said, lowering his jeans to his knees.

I nodded as I quickly unsnapped my button and wiggled my ass, as I pulled them down past my thighs, exposing my pink silk thong. Ricky gave it a passionate rub. "God, you are sexy," he moaned, as he slid my panties down and bent his legs at the knees in an attempt to enter me.

I moved my body as much as I could to meet his erection, as I kept my balance by holding onto the edge of the sink, trying hard not to bang my head again. And then I felt him, and with one hard push, he was inside me. My chest heaved, and I gasped. "Oh yes," I moaned, looking at him with dreamy eyes in the mirror.

Our movements were limited, but the feeling was sensational, like always. With soft strokes and minimal thrusts, Ricky coats the back of my neck with soft kisses as he makes love to me from behind. I stared at him through the mirror and smiled as he continued to stimulate me. We were officially members of the mile-high club. I giggled at the thought.

A loud knock on the door broke our mood.

"Shit," Ricky cussed, as he pulled away from me. "How long have we been in here?"

"A while," I snickered. "We didn't come, but it was awesome," I told him, as I squeezed my body against the sink in an attempt to turn around and face him. I locked my hands around his neck. "I love you so much. Welcome to the club."

Ricky chuckled and struggled to pull up his pants while I continued to have him in a hold. "Who is going out first?"

I lifted my arms carefully above his head to avoid hitting him and slid my panties and jeans up past my legs. "You," I laughed.

Ricky gave himself a quick glance in the mirror and raked his fingers through his hair, pulling it away from his face. He leaned in and gave me a quick kiss on the cheek. "Thanks. I'll see you back at our seats. Just wait a few minutes before coming out."

I nodded and gave his body a little push towards the door. "Go on."

Once Ricky had left, I quickly locked the door again. A few seconds later, another loud knock startled me. "Hold on a minute!" I shouted, unsure if they could hear me over the roaring sounds of the engines. I looked at myself in the mirror and teased my hair before turning to open the door.

I took a deep breath and smiled at the people on the other side. Their eyes were narrowed, and a few shook their heads as I slid by. "It's all yours," I said to the lady at the front of the line, giving her a mischievous grin as I walked away.

I chuckled to myself and was greeted with a loving smile by Ricky as I took my seat next to him, and then it suddenly occurred to me. "Shit."

Ricky turned, his eyes wide. "What?"

I giggled. "I left my bra on the counter in the bathroom, and there is no way I'm going back for it."

Ricky tossed back his head and laughed. "I wonder how many of those end up in the *lost and found* unclaimed?"

CHAPTER 5

By mid-afternoon, we arrived at our favorite hotel, Caesars Palace, in Las Vegas. As I stepped out of the cab, I hooked arms with Ricky and gave him a huge smile. My heart was full. "God, I love this place." I let go of his arm and did a 360 twirl with my arms stretched out, looking up at the sky. The sun welcomed me with its rays of heat and sunshine. I suddenly felt like a Roman empress as I admired the giant, white, majestic horse statues in the entranceway. I had lost count of how many times I had been to Vegas. The playground for adults, as it is known to so many.

My first time was with Sabela, before Slater and Travis, who was once my boyfriend, before he hooked up with Claire. It was a few months after we had met at the dental office. She was the dental assistant, and I was, and still am, the receptionist. On a whim, we came here for the weekend. We were both single and had no plans. I giggled at the memories that suddenly popped into my head. We had gotten so drunk, and I remember now that I lost a lot of money. Sabela had more control than me with gambling. She had two wallets, one had $200, and that was her play money.

Not a penny more, she had insisted. When it's gone, it's gone. And she abided by her rule. In a few hours of our first night, she lost it all and didn't gamble again for the rest of the trip.

On the other hand, I had a credit card from mommy dearest, and I think I blew a couple of grand that weekend. I can't remember what I told my wicked witch of a mother, but whatever it was, she bought it. After all, I was her princess. I cringed at the thought of my mother, happy to be free of her web.

We also met a couple of cute guys at the pool on that trip. I can't for the life of me remember their names. But I remember making out with one of them in the pool after an afternoon of drinking cocktails before we were due to fly out that afternoon. Sabela flirted with the other guy on the sun beds, and I think she may have kissed him a few times. We left the two men horny and tipsy as hell, and barely made our flight home. Shortly after that, she hooked up with the crazy dude Davin, and I met Travis, and we never came back together.

I have been here for wild bachelorette parties, birthday parties, and last Christmas with Ricky, Sadie, and Logan. Oh, it feels so good to be back.

I turned to see Ricky pay the cab driver and grab our luggage and threw him a big smile. "We are here, baby," I squealed.

Ricky took me in his arms and tilted me back until I had one leg stretched out with my toes pointed. He kissed me passionately, almost knocking me off my feet. "Let the fun begin, baby. We are going straight up to our room, so I can rip off all your clothes and celebrate our marriage and you as my wife, Mrs. Ashton."

I gazed into his eyes. "I thought you would never ask," I said, pulling myself back onto my feet. "Let's order champagne and strawberries and eat them under the silk sheets after taking a bubble bath together."

The next morning, the bright sunlight illuminating our room woke me. I smiled and stretched out my arms above my head, enjoying the soft touch of the silk sheets lining my naked body. My full heart could not be altered. After yesterday afternoon and well into the early hours of the morning, I was sexually satisfied and content. This was how honeymoons were meant to be spent. High on champagne and in love, Ricky and I had devoured each other among the plentiful bubbles in the bathtub before moving to the giant king-size bed. We made love many times via the moonlight shining through the windows on the top floor of the hotel. The last thing I remember was being curled in Ricky's arms as we drifted off to sleep, exhausted.

It was then I realized I was in bed alone and heard the water running in the shower. I giggled when I heard Ricky whistling a cheery tune, and then the running water stopped. He had turned off the shower. I missed out on an opportunity to join him. The bathroom door opened a few minutes later, and Ricky entered the room, wearing only a white towel around his waist. I still couldn't believe this gorgeous man chose me to be his wife. Beads of water trickled down his prominent abs. His tanned body glistened from the sunlight, and his radiant smile lit up the room.

"You're awake. How did my beautiful wife sleep?" he said, as he approached the bed.

I watched with lust as he shook his long, drenched hair vigorously close to me and screamed when I was sprayed with cold droplets of water. I sat up and covered myself with the sheets. "Hey, you're getting me all wet."

Ricky laughed, giving his head another good shake before pulling back the sheets and smothering his damp body with mine. "I like it when you're wet," he said, before kissing me hard on the lips.

I found his tongue and sunk my head into the pillows, devouring his mouth and scent. I couldn't get enough of him. After making love all night, I still wanted more and, in haste, yanked the towel away from his body and threw it on the floor. Ricky shifted his body as I spread my legs to welcome him, and in no time, we were celebrating our marriage once again. It didn't take us long to come and after we did, we collapsed into each other's arms as we gasped for air. My chest heaved, and my breaths were loud.

"Are we ever going to leave this room?" I said, as my heart rate slowly returned to normal.

Ricky was still trying to catch his breath and held one arm up against his brow as he laid back against the pillow. "Unless we get dressed in the next five minutes, there is little chance of that happening," he joked.

I jumped out of bed and tugged on Ricky's hand. "Come on, I'm starving. Let's get some breakfast, and then I want to try my luck on the slots. The last time I was here, I won $500" My eyes lit up. "Ooh, then we can go hang out at the Fortuna Pool. They have a blackjack table right in the water. We couldn't pull Sadie away from it over Christmas. Do you remember?"

Ricky laughed. "I do. But she ended up coming out ahead, if I recall."

"Yeah, she sure did, but lost it all that night in the casino."

Ricky nudged my arm and cracked a laugh. "May I remind you that you lost all your winnings, too?"

I returned the nudge. "Well, that's because you didn't stop me. It's all your fault." I jumped off the bed and skipped across the room to my suitcase and began flinging clothes on the bed. "Come on, let's get out of here. All this gambling talk is making me want to waste more money."

CHAPTER 6

Standing in the enormous, loud and busy casino room with aisles of slot machines, I soon forgot about breakfast. I scanned the room and grinned when a machine lit up, announcing it had a winner.

It was only ten o'clock in the morning, and the room was bustling with gamblers. Cocktail waitresses were hustling, selling morning alcohol drinks, and cigarette smoke filled the air as it floated and circled in front of the hundreds of flashing lights.

I had such a rush as I watched an older woman to my left scream when her machine lit up. The sound of money dropping into an imaginary tray played through the speakers as her playing card loaded up with her winnings.

"I won $100," she yelled, while clapping her hands vigorously in the air. I giggled at her with happiness and reached into my purse for my wallet. I handed Ricky a hundred-dollar bill. "Honey, go get me a playing card."

"What about breakfast? I'm starving."

"Oh, just five minutes," I whined, while shaking the C-Note in front of him.

Ricky's jaw dropped. "You better not lose all that in five minutes. We'll be broke before lunchtime."

I laughed. "No, I hope to double it. Now go on. I'm going to watch people play until you get back. Maybe someone else will win."

Ricky shook his head in defeat as he took the money and headed to the cashier's window, which was in clear view of where I stood.

After he left, my fingers itched to play the machines, and I anxiously waited for his return. The lady that had just won was still sitting at the same machine, constantly pushing buttons, hoping for another win. Another scream, followed by laughter, caught my attention. This time, it came from behind me. I turned and saw two young females locked in a dance while their machine made the familiar winning sounds. I laughed out loud and gave them a thumbs up.

Ricky finally returned and handed me the card. "I'm off to get a bloody Mary. Do you want one?"

I gave him a quick nod as I headed over to the nearest machine.

"Stay right here, otherwise, I will never find you."

I gave him another nod as I fed my card into the machine and placed my bet.

My smile soon disappeared when I was down $25 in less than five minutes. I turned my head in search of Ricky. He was nowhere in sight. "Come on, Ricky, this machine sucks. I want to move someplace else," I moaned under my breath. Suddenly, the man sitting at the machine next to me stood and left. Before anyone else had a chance, I quickly left my losing machine and dashed over to the now-empty seat, which was still warm. I shifted in the chair for the most comfortable position and smiled when I found it.

I patted the top metal rim of the flashing machine and spoke to it. "Ok, buddy. I need some luck sent my way. Show me what you got." A few minutes later, I still wasn't feeling it. I was down another $10 "Damn it," I hissed under my breath before a hand on my shoulder startled me.

Ricky's warm breath coated my ear when he spoke. "How are you doing? Win anything yet?"

After giving him a quick glance, my eyes quickly returned to the slot machine as I gave him an abrupt reply. "No." I placed another bet. "It's gotta pay off soon."

Ricky laughed and placed his hands on his hips. "The voice of a gambler. Come on, I'm starving. Let's get something to eat. You can play some more afterward."

I brushed him away with my elbow before reaching for the bloody Mary he had set on the machine. "In a minute. I have a good feeling about this one."

"You have a good feeling about every machine you sit at," Ricky joked.

I continued to play while Ricky looked on, but after I was down another $10. I was ready to call it quits and hit the button one more time. "Okay, the last one, I promise."

"About time. You know this is husband abuse, right? Keeping him from eating breakfast. I'm so hungry."

I wasn't paying attention and simply nodded as I watched the numbers spin in front of me. And then it happened as soon as the last number landed. The machine lit up and the flashing light on top illuminated red. Loud music blasted from the speakers, and the glorious sound effects of coins dropping filled my ears as the machine paid my card. "Shit! I won. Ricky, I won," I squealed, while raising my hands.

Ricky quickly leaned in and watched the total of my card continue to increase. "Shit, you are at $200. How much did you win?"

My eyes bulged. "I have no idea."

The machine continued to pay out. I looked behind me and saw a few people had stopped to watch.

"I'm at $500 now. Holy shit."

We continued to watch, as my card value continued to rise and the beautiful sound effect of money dropping in a tray continued to play. More people had gathered around us, cheering as I clapped my hands and squealed louder, "$2,000 Ricky!"

"And it's still adding money!" Ricky roared.

"I know. I told you I had a good feeling about this machine. Happy honeymoon, baby," I yelled, jumping up and throwing myself into his arms.

"How much did you win?" an older lady standing close to us asked.

"I have no idea. It's still paying out," I said, while beaming a huge

smile.

"$4,000 now," Ricky hollered, with wide eyes.

"Fuck. I've never won more than $500 at a time. This is insane," I said, while fixing my eyes on the machine.

A cocktail waitress stopped and smiled. "Congratulations honey. Can I get you a drink to celebrate?"

Still locked in Ricky's arms, I shook my head and held up my bloody Mary. "No thanks. We are good."

When $5,000 had been added to my card, the deafening sounds and music ceased on the machine. The sound of money dropping also stopped. "Wow! I won $5,000," I screamed.

"Welcome to Vegas, baby," I yelled to Ricky, as the large crowd that now surrounded us cheered on.

Ricky pulled me into his arms and gave me a long, drawn-out kiss. "I don't friggin' believe it."

He picked me up and spun me around. I laughed as I landed on my feet. "I'm buying breakfast."

Ricky reached in front of me and grabbed my card from the slot. "Let's cash in first."

"But I may want to play some more."

Ricky grabbed my hand. "Which is why I want to cash in before you blow it all. I'll leave a couple of hundred on the card."

"But I don't want all that cash in my purse."

Ricky headed towards the cashier while holding onto my hand. "We can put it in the safe in our room after we have eaten."

He turned and winked. "Besides, it will give us an excuse to return to our room and celebrate our marriage one more time."

CHAPTER 7

Over breakfast, cuddled in a booth, Ricky and I continued to be in shock over my winnings. We periodically shook our heads in disbelief and broke out in bursts of laughter over our good fortune, in between bites of our food.

"I still can't believe it. This will pay for all the shows you want to see and our meals all week," Ricky said with a huge grin.

"And when I play more on the slots," I added, before grabbing the check off the table. "Come on, let's go stash this money and fool around some more. All this cash is making me horny," I laughed.

Ricky pulled me in close. "You and I both. Come on, let's get out of here."

After paying the check, I didn't hesitate to pursue Ricky out of the restaurant. The main lobby was more crowded and noisier than when we left. It amazes me every time how many people they draw to this sin city, and how much money they spend here. My $5,000 winning was nothing compared to what this place was making by the hour.

Ricky grabbed my hand and led me through the crowd of people that were standing around the slot machines and blackjack tables. We spotted an open elevator and raced to catch it. When we were about twenty feet away from it, the doors began to close and we found ourselves staring at a pretty young girl standing inside the elevator, dressed in a super sexy long, black dress, with one side of the shoulder bare and a slit up to her thigh. Standing next to her was a middle-aged man with short dark hair, wearing a business suit. He whispered in her ear, which told me they were together.

Ricky and I both knew we weren't going to make it to the elevator and stopped in our tracks. Ricky stared at the woman in the black dress, and his eyes grew enormous. His hand fell from my grip as he spoke. "Annie?"

The elevator doors closed as I looked at Ricky with a furrowed brow. "What?"

Still in a daze, he repeated her name. "That was my sister Annie."

I repeated myself. "What? Are you sure? I thought you said she lived in Los Angeles with some loser."

"She does. Or the last I heard, she did. I know that was Annie. I should know my own sister when I see her."

I reached out and rested my hand on his arm. "You haven't seen her in over three years. Are you sure that was her?"

Ricky raised his hand to his brow. A look of confusion smeared his face. "Yes, I'm sure. What is she doing here? And who was that guy whispering in her ear?"

"That guy in the elevator sure didn't look like a loser to me. I honestly don't think it was her, Ricky. I think you are mistaken."

Ricky freed his arm from my hand where it had been resting and raised his voice. "How would you know, Jill? You've never met her. Are you telling me I don't know what my sister looks like? I'm telling you, that was her. I am one hundred percent certain. There is no doubt in my mind. That was Annie, and I want to know what the hell she is doing in Vegas, and yet, she couldn't come to our wedding?"

I glanced around the area where we stood and saw that people were watching us as they walked by. "Ricky, keep your voice down. People are staring at us."

"Let them stare. We are talking about my sister. Someone who is too busy to come to her brother's wedding, yet has time to party it up in Vegas. A sister who is supposed to be broke." Suddenly, he pulled his phone out of his pants pocket. "I'm going to call her right now." He released a sarcastic laugh. "Boy, she has mom fooled. Mom is paying for her phone." Ricky hastily searched his phone and made the call. "I got her voice mail," he hissed, before leaving a message, using a sharp tone. "Hey Annie, it's your brother here, Ricky. I just saw you in Vegas at Caesars Palace, where Jill and I are spending our honeymoon. Call me." Ricky hung up his phone and returned it to his pocket.

Even though I had never met Annie, I still wasn't convinced that was her. Things weren't adding up. "If that was Annie, then who was the guy she was with? Do you think she might be having an affair?" I asked Ricky.

"I don't know. But if she is, it's pretty chicken shit that she'd much rather see some dude in Vegas than come to our wedding."

"Maybe she had a good reason," I suggested, attempting to calm Ricky down.

"It better be a damn good one. Wish I knew what room she was in. I'd go bang on her door right now." He grabbed my hand. "Come on, I need a drink. I'm going to figure out what is going on and sort this out. Annie is hiding something."

CHAPTER 8

I sat across from Ricky at the small, round black table in the bar. My nerves peaked, and I was at a loss for words, fearing that whatever I might say may add to his anger. Ricky sat in silence, his nostrils flared, as he chugged down a shot of tequila and chased it down with a beer. Sweat beaded on his brow. I knew it wasn't from the bright lights in the bar. He was tense, and his anger was building. He needed answers, and I still needed confirmation that the woman we saw was Annie, even though Ricky had made it clear he was convinced it was her.

The music in the bar was loud, as were the people around us. A waitress approached our table, and Ricky spoke to her in a sharp tone without making eye contact. "Bring us two more rounds."

The waitress nodded and scurried away.

"Ricky, I haven't even finished my first one yet."

He wiped his mouth with his sleeve and rolled his eyes. "Well, I'm ready for another one," he confessed, as he scanned the bar. "And it might be a while before the waitress makes it back to our table, so I ordered two more."

I shifted in my seat. "It's not like you to drink this much during the day."

"Well, it's not exactly a normal day, Jill. I just saw my damn sister in Vegas when she is supposed to be struggling in Los Angeles. Not only that, she is with some dude that her own brother doesn't know about," he snarled.

I hesitated before speaking. "We don't know for sure if it is her, Ricky."

Ricky's eyes narrowed as he glared at me from across the table. His elbows rested on the wooden surface as he leaned in closer to me. The smell of alcohol was trapped in his breath. "Trust me, that was Annie. I'm not going to tell you again."

I returned to my silent state as I watched Ricky chug down another shot that the waitress had just dropped off. I had never seen him vent such anger before, and wasn't sure how to react. Disappointment set in. "Ricky, we are supposed to be on our honeymoon. Let's try to have a good time."

He rolled his eyes again, took a swig of his beer, and smacked his lips before speaking. "Jill, we will resume our honeymoon after I find out why my sister is in Vegas."

"Well, how do you plan on doing that? We have no idea which room she is in, or who the man is that she is with. If that is her, I might add."

"I don't know, but I'm going to find out, even if I have to sit here all night and wait for her to come down to the lobby again. She can't stay in her room forever."

I gave him a sarcastic laugh. "Well, that's a stupid plan. There is more than one elevator in this hotel. Even I know that. She could have left by now for all we know."

"Well, do you have a better idea?"

His question caught me off guard. "Well, no. But sitting here getting drunk isn't going to solve anything, and it's ruining our honeymoon."

Ricky replied with another tequila shot. "I need to think, okay.

The honeymoon is not ruined. I just need to figure this out and find out what's going on."

After his third shot and three beer chasers, Ricky's eyes appeared glassy and his body swayed slightly from side to side. He raised his hand to get the waitress' attention. I reached up and grabbed it in an attempt to pull it down. "I think you've had enough, Ricky," I told him.

Ricky pulled his arm away from my hold. "I'll tell you when I've had enough."

The waitress stood at our table and Ricky pointed to our empty glasses. "Bring us two more rounds."

After she had left, I spoke to Ricky in a sharp tone. "Damn it, Ricky, I don't want to spend my honeymoon in a friggin' bar watching you get drunk."

"I'm not getting drunk, Jill. I'm just having a few drinks to calm me down. Aren't you pissed my sister came to Vegas instead of our wedding? Because I sure as hell am … "

"If I knew it was her for certain, then yes, I would be upset." I raised my hand before Ricky could cut me off. "Yes, I know you've already told me it was definitely her. I don't know that for sure, and until I do, I'm not going to assume anything. You should do the same."

The waitress reappeared at our table, and Ricky quickly grabbed a beer. "Fine, but I know I am right and I will prove it to you."

CHAPTER 9

I was relieved to see my words had calmed Ricky down a little and reached across the table to rest my hand on his. "Do you want to do something to take our minds off all of this?"

Ricky squeezed my hand, which made me feel better. His anger was subsiding. "I'm sorry, babe, for getting upset and ruining our honeymoon. Annie has a lot of explaining to do, and I won't rest until she does. I know it's none of my business what she does with her life. Hell, we've not seen each other in years. I hardly know her, but she obviously lied to me about why she couldn't come to our wedding. That's what I'm angry about. I hate being lied to. Especially by my own sister. You just don't do that."

I caressed the top of his hand as I spoke. "I know, baby. If it's her, I'm sure she has a good explanation."

"She'd better have." Ricky pushed the remaining glasses away. "Come on. Let's get out of here."

I smiled. "Do you want to go catch a show? The Blue Man Group is playing here. We've been wanting to see them."

Ricky stood and held out his hand, which I happily took.

"Sounds like a good idea." He pulled me in and kissed me. "I'm sorry, and I won't let Annie ruin our honeymoon. I love you."

"I love you too. We will somehow sort this out. After the show, do you mind if I play the slots again?"

Ricky threw back his head and laughed. "Sure, but I think you might have a bit of a gambling problem," he joked.

I slapped his chest. "No, I don't. It's just fun."

"Yeah, until you lose all your money."

"Well, I'm up $5,000. I haven't lost any yet," I said with sarcasm. I suddenly came to an abrupt stop. "Oh shit, the money is still in my purse."

Ricky yanked on my hand. "We'll take it up to the room after the show.

I think it starts soon."

∼

It was a good idea to have the Blue Man Group entertain us. Once the show started, Ricky held me tight, laughed, and moved his body to the beat of the music, soon forgetting about Annie.

He opted to drink iced tea when the waitress asked for our order, which pleased me, and by the time the show was over, any signs Ricky had of being tipsy or angry had disappeared. He was back to his normal, happy self. We were back on track with our honeymoon.

When we reached the lobby, I checked my phone and saw that I had missed a text from Sabela, and my mom had left me a voice-mail. I was more concerned about the text from Sabela. "Crap, Sabela texted me," I said out loud, while opening the message.

Ricky came to an abrupt halt and let go of my hand. "What did she say? Is Slater okay?"

"Hold on," I said, as I pulled up her message and read it out loud. "Hey guys, I just wanted to let you know Slater came home today. He is doing great and sends you his love. We hope you are having a great time. Call us when you get back." Ricky and I released a huge sigh of relief.

"Thank god," Ricky said, with his hand up to his chest. "I was worried there for a minute."

"Me too. I guess my mom called while we were watching the show. She left me a message."

"What did she say?" Ricky asked.

I shut off my phone and slid it into my purse. "I don't know. I didn't listen to it."

Ricky creased his brow. "Really? Maybe she apologized."

I folded my arms and leaned back in my chair. "Yeah, that would be just like her. Apologize in a voicemail when she is 6,000 miles away. I honestly don't want to hear her voice right now. Especially on my honeymoon. It's bad enough with Annie pissing you off." The minute I said her name, I regretted it. For the last two hours, she had been out of his head, and now I had to go put my foot in my mouth and say her name. "Shit, I didn't mean to bring her up again. I'm sorry."

Ricky gave a slight nod. "It's okay. It still bothers me, and I will find out what's going on before we leave Vegas. We are not leaving until we do."

I rested my hand on his arm. "I'm not sure how, Ricky. Did she ever return your call?"

Ricky shook his head. "Nope. I've checked many times. That's not like her either. She usually gets back to me within an hour or two."

"Well, what do you want to do?" I asked, not sure of his mood.

Ricky smiled, which put me at ease, and wrapped his arms around my waist before spinning me around. I giggled as he kissed me tenderly on the lips. "Well, you don't want to talk to your mom, and I don't want to dwell on Annie right now. Let's say we forget about family and spend the afternoon by the pool, sipping cocktails and playing some pool blackjack." He gave me a huge, sexy grin. "I could lather you up with oil and caress every inch of your body."

I pulled him in closer and gave him a long, drawn out kiss. "Hmm, I like that idea. Let's go up to our room and change."

Ricky took my hand. "Lead the way, pretty lady."

It didn't take us long to change and within the hour, we were at the Fortuna Pool. The only pool at the hotel where you could laze in the water and play blackjack at the table surrounded by concrete stools in the middle of the pool. Here, the party never ended, no matter what time of day or night it was. It was only around two in the afternoon, and the place was jumping with loud music, cocktails being served by waitresses in swimsuits, and a crowd trying their luck at the Blackjack table. Ricky had called down ahead of time, and was lucky to have been able to reserve a cabana. He waved over a cute brunette holding a silver tray and gave her his name.

After ordering two glasses of white wine, Ricky slid the two lounge beds together. "We are on our honeymoon. I want to lie next to you. Not two feet away."

I laughed at his cute gesture, and slipped out of my white lace wrap that covered my tiny pink bikini.

Ricky's jaw dropped. "Damn, you look hot. Why have I never seen that bikini before?"

I giggled. "I bought it especially for our honeymoon. Do you like it?" I asked in a flirtatious manner, as I gave him a sexy pose.

"Like it. I love it. You wear it well. It doesn't leave much to the imagination." He took me in his arms and kissed me hard on the lips. "God, I'm a lucky man."

I kissed him back as I ran my hands through his long strands of hair. "And I'm a lucky woman. Come on, let's go in the pool and then we can come back here and you can oil me up. I want to bake in the sun and sip on fine wine."

The water was the perfect temperature, refreshing and relaxing. After smooching in each other's arms amongst the crowd around us, Ricky played a few hands of blackjack, but lost each time. "I guess you are the lucky winner when it comes to gambling. I quit," Ricky said, as he swam away from the table.

A rush of panic swept through me. "Oh, shoot."

"What?"

"I forgot to put my winnings in the safe when we went up to our room."

"Oh crap, and I forgot to remind you." He looked around the pool. "Where's your purse?"

I pointed to our cabana. "Under my towel on the lounge chair."

"Shit Jill, you can't just leave it anywhere."

I gave him a sarcastic stare. "Well, I can't exactly take it in the pool with me, now can I?"

He held out his hand. "Come on, let's go back to our spot. I want to make sure your purse is still there. That would really ruin our honeymoon if it's gone."

I rolled my eyes, feeling confident it would be. There's too many people around for anyone to steal it. I took his hand. "I'm sure it's still there, Ricky. Look at all these people around us."

He yanked on my hand. "I just want to make sure. Besides, it's a good excuse to rub some oil on you," he added with a wink.

Back at the cabana, Ricky wasted no time pulling back my towel on the lounge chair and released a huge breath of relief when he saw my pink leather purse, untouched.

"Thank god," he said with a smile, as he picked it up and checked the contents. "The money is still there."

"I told you it would be fine," I said with a smirk, as he handed me my purse and then moved our chairs into the sun. After making sure the zipper to my purse was closed, I placed it under my lounge chair before getting comfortable and laying on my stomach. "Come on, why don't you put some oil on my back and come lay down next to me," I said, as I untied the strings to my bikini top and let them fall free.

Ricky didn't need to be asked twice, and immediately reached for the oil in our bag and poured a puddle in the middle of my back. I moaned when I felt his powerful hands kneading the oil into my skin. My body relaxed from the strength of his deep rubs and the warmth of the sun. I closed my eyes and thought about Annie again, and wondered if that was who we saw. I suddenly wanted to know. Earlier, it didn't really bother me. I was more upset over Ricky's anger. I was sure he was mistaken, but now I was not so sure. He's convinced it was her and is now refusing to leave Vegas until he finds her. As much as I don't want to admit it, and as hard as I am trying to put her out of my mind and not let her haunt our honeymoon, I'm finding I can't. I concluded that we would not be able to enjoy our honeymoon until we found out if the woman was Annie. Our honeymoon won't begin until we do.

CHAPTER 10

I must have drifted off to sleep, because I woke to the sound of Ricky whispering in my ear.

"Hey Jill, wake up. Your back is getting fried."

I squinted, looking up while blocking the sun out of my eyes. "What?"

"Your back is burned. You need to go inside."

I rubbed my eyes and suddenly remembered where I was. "Shoot. How long have I been asleep?"

"Probably an hour."

I quickly sat up and felt the tightness of my skin on my back from the sunburn. "Shit, Ricky, why did you let me fall asleep? Now I'm going to be stinging."

Ricky raised his hands. "Hey don't blame me. I fell asleep too. Probably from drinking alcohol during the day."

I pulled myself up while discreetly tying the strings to my bikini. I turned my back to face Ricky. "Is it really red?" I asked with concern.

Ricky sat up and pressed down on my skin. "Oh yeah, you are burned, sweetie. You are going to be stinging later."

"Damn it." I turned and smacked his shoulder. "It's not funny. I hate getting a sunburn. It takes all the fun out of everything."

Ricky laughed. "Oh, come on. It won't be that bad. I'll take care of you." He took my hand. "Come on, grab your stuff and let's go inside." He handed me my wrap. "Here, put this on and cover yourself up. We will go up to our room, put that damn money in the safe, and order some room service."

I gave him a sweet kiss on the lips. "Let's cuddle on the bed and watch old black and white movies."

Ricky smiled and took my hand. "Deal."

We held hands as we walked through the massive lobby of the hotel. The familiar sound of slot machines being played and winning bells going off filled my ears. We walked close together, dodging people in our path and occasionally bumping shoulders as we made our way to the elevators. Suddenly, Ricky came to an abrupt stop and stared across the room.

"Shit, that's the guy."

I glanced over to where his eyes were focused but drew a blank. "What guy?"

"The guy that was with Annie. That's him."

I looked again. "Are you sure?"

Ricky raised his voice. "Yes. I'm positive. That is the dude that was with Annie in the elevator." He let go of my hand. "I'm going to go talk to him right now."

I quickly pulled him back. "Hold on a second, Ricky. You can't just go barging over there. He's at one of those high roller tables. The casino may throw us out for causing a scene. Act calm. Let's just hang out close by and wait for him to leave the table."

"That might take all night. Look at him. He looks like a prick, don't you think? Standing there smoking a cigar with a pile of chips in front of him, acting like he owns the place."

"Well, he must be pretty rich to be playing at one of those tables."

"Are you sure you just don't want to go over there?" Ricky said again.

I yanked on his arm. "No, I don't. We are going to wait until he leaves. I don't want you causing a scene." I pulled on his arm with more force. "Come on. There is a bar close by where we can watch him. I need to get something to eat, too. I'm starving. Hopefully, they will serve food."

We were lucky enough to find a table that had a good view of where the man was playing. I sat down first and looked his way. He was laughing and chewing on a cigar as he raked in more chips from the center of the table. His gold watch, which I assumed was a Rolex, glistened beneath the lights of the gambling table, and his gray suit glimmered.

"Man, everything he is wearing is expensive," I said to Ricky, who was also looking at him. "I bet he's loaded," I added.

"How old do you think he is?" Ricky asked.

I shrugged my shoulders. "I dunno. Maybe in his mid-40s, early 50s."

Ricky slouched back in his chair and took a swig of the beer that had just arrived. "I wonder how my sister knows him?"

"We still don't know for sure if it was your sister."

Ricky ignored my comment. "Surely she can't be having an affair with him? He's gotta be twice her age unless he's kicking her down some money." He shook his head. "Nah, that can't be it. She's always telling our mom how she's struggling and working all the time. That's why mom pays for her cellphone." Ricky pulled his phone out of his pocket and checked his voicemails. "She never returned my call. What the hell is going on with her?"

After Ricky finished rambling on with all his unanswered questions, I pulled my phone out of my purse and opened the text app. "I miss Maggie. I'm going to text Sadie and see how she's doing. Poor puppy is probably wondering where we are." After I had sent the text, I waited anxiously for Sadie to reply, hoping she had her phone close by. "It's Monday. She's probably at work. I hope Maggie is okay by herself."

Ricky smirked. "I'm sure she is okay. She's fine when we go to work and leave her alone all day."

"I know, but she is in a strange place." My phone suddenly pinged, and I quickly picked it up and read Sadie's text out loud. "Maggie is doing great. She is so gosh darn cute. I may never give her back." I laughed and continued to read out loud. "Me and Logan take her for a walk every night after dinner. I don't know why, but I think it's really romantic. We hold hands and look at the moon. It's awesome. We are even talking about getting a dog now, all because we love our evening walks with Maggie. It's all your fault LOL. How's the honeymoon going? Miss you guys." I texted her a quick reply, letting her know we were having a good time, and decided not to mention anything about Ricky's sister. "Aww, that's so cool. They may get a dog because they've been having so much fun taking care of Maggie. I wonder what they will get?" I told Ricky.

Ricky wasn't paying attention. He was engrossed watching the guy at the table and simply nodded. "Yeah, that's cool," he said, while not looking my way.

I folded my arms and leaned back in my chair while glancing over my shoulder. "Where is our food? I'm so hungry, and chilly, too. I need to change out of this bikini and wrap."

Ricky didn't answer and gave me another nod.

"Ricky, are you listening to me? I feel like I'm talking to myself."

"Yes, I'm listening, but I'm also watching the dude at the table. I don't want him to leave and disappear. He is my only link to Annie."

I smiled when the waitress arrived, and couldn't wait to dig into my fish and chips. Ricky didn't even acknowledge the bacon cheeseburger that was placed in front of him. I didn't wait for Ricky to start eating, and chowed down my food in haste.

"Damn you are hungry, slow down, you're going to make yourself sick," Ricky said, before taking a bite of his burger, and then continued to stare at the guy while he ate his meal. I discovered that trying to have a conversation with him was pointless, and ate in silence while periodically glancing over to where the guy sat. "I wonder how much money he has in chips? He has a lot stacked in front of him." I suddenly gasped. "Oh shit, he's standing. Looks like he is done playing. Look, some guy is taking his chips."

"I see that," Ricky quickly stood. "Come on. I don't want to lose him."

"What about the check?"

"They have our room number. They will bill it. Come on, let's go. He's leaving the table."

I grabbed my purse. "I'm coming. Hold on a second. Geez."

Ricky grabbed my hand and quickened his pace while I struggled to keep up. Thank god I was wearing sandals that had a low heel. Not taking his eyes off the guy, Ricky shuffled between the crowd while I struggled to walk fast. We could still see him and it looked like he was heading towards the nearby bar. Now that we knew where he was going, Ricky slowed down, much to my relief, as I took a few deep breaths.

When we entered the bar, Ricky let go of my hand and scanned the area. I did the same and spotted him sitting at the bar talking to the pretty brunette bartender. "I see him. He's at the bar," I said in Ricky's ear.

"I see him too. Come on. Don't take your eyes off him."

Ricky reached him first and gave him a gentle tap on the shoulder, while I stood behind him, my heart hammering against my chest.

"Excuse me, can I talk to you for a second?" Ricky asked the guy.

The man slowly turned around and gave Ricky a puzzled look, and seemed to look down at him. His voice was stiff and sounded arrogant when he spoke. "Do I know you?" He glanced over

Ricky's shoulder and gave me the once over. I quickly focused my eyes on the bottles of booze behind the bar.

"No, you don't, but I saw you with my sister earlier today. How do you know her and what were you doing with her?"

The man leaned back in his chair and took a big puff of his cigar. He took his time to answer and exhaled puffs of smoke towards Ricky's face. "I think you are mistaken, young man."

"See, I told you it wasn't her, Ricky." I rested my hand on his shoulder. "Come on, let's go."

Ricky gave his shoulder a hard shake and waved his hand at the invasive smoke circling in front of his face. "I'm not leaving until this guy tells me the truth." He narrowed his lips and glared at the man. His tone was sharp. "I know I saw you with my sister. Her name is Annie. I want to know what you were doing with her?"

The man gave Ricky a demoralizing smirk. "And I told you that you are mistaken. I am married for god sakes, and have four children. Please, leave me alone."

"That means nothing. Where are your wife and kids? I don't see them here," Ricky snarled.

"I don't have to answer to you," the man replied, and took a swig of his scotch that the bartender had just placed in front of him.

Ricky pulled out two empty chairs next to him and gave me a stare. "Have a seat, Jill. It's a public bar. Let's have a couple of drinks." He turned and spat out his next words to the guy. "I will follow you everywhere, even camp outside your room, until you tell me what you were doing with my sister. I'm not going away. You owe me an explanation. You were with Annie, and I want to know why."

CHAPTER 11

I couldn't help noticing how uncomfortable the man looked as Ricky and I took our seats and ordered two drinks. I watched as the man gulped down his scotch and raised his hand to the bartender for another one. He coughed before he spoke. I wasn't sure if it was from the burn of alcohol in his throat or his nerves.

"Look, I don't know who the hell you are, but I told you, I am married. I have no idea who your sister is. I have a wife, and I am here on business."

Ricky didn't cower. "Oh, so your wife is not even here. You are alone? How often do you come to Vegas alone? Does your wife know what you do in Vegas?" Ricky cracked a laugh, folding his arms across his chest and smirking at the guy. "Oh. that's right, what happens in Vegas stays in Vegas."

The guy spat out his next words. "Look, punk, I have just had about enough of you. What is it you want? Money?"

"Oh, so now you are trying to bribe me to stay quiet, which tells me you were with my sister. Otherwise, why would you try to keep me quiet? Which is what I am assuming you are trying to do?" Ricky stood to his feet, putting my nerves on edge. He was fired up, and I didn't know what he would do next. He came within inches of the guy's face and spat out his words. "You think I'm a punk, eh? Well, how about this punk starts a scene and draws attention to our little conversation? I have nothing to lose, but I sure as hell bet you do. I know your type. Let me guess, you probably told your wife you were off on some business trip in New York or LA, and instead, you snuck off to Vegas. Maybe if I cause enough commotion, I'll get us on TV. What do you say, big shot?"

The guy failed to hide his nerves and glanced around the bar. He whispered in a sharp tone, "Will you please sit down? The woman I was with was not your sister. Her name wasn't Annie. Now will you please leave me alone?" he hissed.

Ricky spat back. "And I'm telling you, she was my sister. Maybe she gave you another name. At least tell me how you know her and where I can find her, or I swear to god, I will make sure your wife hears about your little trip to Vegas via the local news."

The man breathed more heavily, and his cheeks swelled as his nostrils flared. "I don't know her, okay? She works for an escort service. I found her on their website. Now leave me alone."

Ricky's eyes lit up. "An escort service? You mean she's a prostitute?"

The man shook his head. "I don't like to use that word. She accompanied me to a table and then we went to my suite for an hour. I'll probably never see her again."

Ricky shook his head. "Annie is a prostitute? What the fuck?" He gave the guy a hard stare. "What name did she give you?"

"I don't remember."

Ricky curled his hand into a fist and gave the guy a good hit on the shoulder. "Think, god damn it! We are talking about my sister."

The guy raised his hand to his brow that was now sweating profusely. "I'm not sure. Carie. Karen. Carina." He looked up with bright eyes. "Carina! That's it. Her name was Carina."

"And what website did you find her on?" Ricky barked.

"The one I always use. Vegas twenty-four hours.com."

Ricky turned to me and gave me a sharp look. "Write that down, Jill."

I fumbled in my purse for my phone, and immediately typed the name in my notes app. "Got it," I said, after returning my phone to my purse.

The guy straightened his tie and dusted off his suit where Ricky had thumped him. "Are we done here?"

"Yeah, I got what I needed." He gave his shoulder a hard nudge. "Hey, say hi to the Mrs, and kids." Ricky turned and looked at me. "Come on Jill, let's go."

Feeling relieved, I gave Ricky a faint smile and followed his lead. "Where are we going?"

"To book a girl called Carina and have her come to our room in about an hour. If I can't go to her, she can come to us."

CHAPTER 12

I was relieved when we got back to our room. My skin itched and felt dry from the chlorine in the pool. I couldn't wait to get in the shower. As soon as Ricky opened the door, I threw my purse on the bed and headed for the bathroom, leaving a trail of my clothes on the floor behind me as I undressed on the way. "I'll be right out. My arms itch like crazy," I hollered from across the room.

Ricky looked up. "You got some sun. How is your sunburn?"

I stopped just before I entered the bathroom and looked at my shoulder. It was pink, but thankfully no blisters. "To be honest, I forgot all about it when we went to the bar and you had it out with that guy. But now I'm itching." I paused. "You never got his name, did you?"

Ricky shook his head. "Nah. Not important." He pulled his phone out from his back pocket and sat on the bed. "Hurry up so we can set up this fake date with Miss Carina," he said, with a heavy tone of sarcasm.

I looked over my shoulder again and gave him a flirtatious smile before giving him a sexy wink. "Can I talk you into rubbing me all over with some after sun cream? I don't want to peel or sting."

Ricky looked my way and grinned. "You don't have to ask me twice. Better yet, why don't I join you in the shower and soap you up? I'll be gentle, I promise," he added with a smile.

After a brief session of caressing and kissing, Ricky kept his promise and was gentle, lathering me up with soap, and even taking the time to wash my hair before coating my body with a refreshing moisturizer.

Once we had returned to the bed dressed in our white fluffy bathrobes, Ricky reached over to the nightstand and grabbed the complimentary notepad and pen, and made himself comfortable against the pillows. Between us was his phone. "Okay, let's look up that site. What was it called again?"

I grabbed my phone off the nightstand, and located it in my notes and read it out loud, "Vegas twenty-four hours.com"

Ricky entered it on his phone and we both stared at the screen, waiting anxiously for the site to load. When it did, the page was covered with images of beautiful women and the words, "Available Now," were written across the bottom of each photo.

"Do you see her?" I asked, as Ricky scrolled down the page.

He shook his head. "I wonder if I can search by name?"

"You may have to register first. Look there, on the top left. It says, "Open an account."

Ricky tossed his head back onto the pillow. "Shit, I don't want to give my real name."

"I'm sure most people don't. You can probably make up a username, but your credit card info will have to be legit. I'm sure she doesn't see all that. Just the people that run the site and whoever she is working for," I told him.

"Okay, let's do this. I'll register an account and then we will see if we can find her. She has to be here. The guy said it's where he found her."

It took us about twenty minutes to get everything set up and enter Ricky's credit card information. "I wonder how much this is going to cost. Any idea what the going rate is?" Ricky asked.

I creased my brow. "How would I know?"

After they approved his credit card, the screen changed to a page titled *Membership Lounge*.

Ricky rubbed his hands together. "Ooh, we are in the lounge now." He scanned the screen. "Okay, how do we search for a girl?"

I touched the screen. "Up there under search."

Ricky typed in the name Carina and waited. Within seconds, the girl who we had seen in the elevator appeared on the screen.

Ricky's jaw dropped, and he sat up. "That's Annie."

I looked at the girl. "Are you sure?"

"Yes. That is my sister. I knew it. I knew it was her. What is she doing?" He looked up in a daze. "Jill, Annie is working for an escort service. Why?"

I rested my hand on his arm. "Ricky, we will get to the bottom of this. Book her and we will ask her all those questions when she comes here."

Ricky handed me his phone. "Can you do it? It feels really weird booking my sister for an hour of what is supposed to be sex."

I took his phone. "Sure."

After going through the process and availability times, I looked over at Ricky, who had been quiet the whole time. "It says she is available in two hours. Do you want me to reserve it?"

Ricky nodded. "Yes. The sooner I can talk to her, the better."

Within a few clicks, I received the confirmation. "Done. She will be here at 8:00 PM."

For the next hour, we discussed a plan. We needed to have her enter the room and keep her there before she realized the man was Ricky. We decided the door would be open a crack, with me standing behind it against the wall. Ricky would have his back to the door, looking out the window. When she knocked, he would yell its open and tell her to come in. I would then immediately close it once she was in the middle of the room, blocking her from leaving.

"Do you think this will work?" Ricky asked with uncertainty.

"It has to. I can't think of another way to keep her in the room and talk to us. Can you?"

Ricky wiped his sweaty palms on his robe and stood up from the bed. "Okay then. I'm going to get dressed and have a few shots from the wet bar before she arrives."

My nerves matched Ricky's. "I'll get dressed too and join you with those shots."

Ten minutes prior to Annie's arrival, I tried to have Ricky sit down, who had been pacing the room for some time. "You need to calm down, Ricky. I'm sure she has a good explanation for everything."

"I can't. I have so many questions for her. I can't believe my sister is a hooker in Las Vegas. How did she even get into this?"

"Well, the site actually says escort service."

Ricky gave a sarcastic laugh. "Oh come on Jill, we both know that's an upper class word for hooker. She has sex for money."

I checked my phone for the time. "She should be here in a few minutes. We need to get in position." I laughed at my words. "God, I sound like a detective." I pointed to the window. "Go stand over there and I will crack the door open." I waited while Ricky did as I asked, then walked over to the door and opened it. I then took my place against the wall.

A few minutes later, I could hear footsteps off in the distance down the hallway that seemed to get closer. "I think she is coming," I whispered across the room, and then held my breath.

The footsteps were definitely getting closer. I tried to control my heavy breathing, which I feared she would hear. A few seconds later, there was a knock at the door.

"It's open. Come in," Ricky called, right on cue, loud enough to be heard.

Holding my breath, I watched as someone slowly pushed the door open and pressed my body hard against the wall so as not to be hit by it.

A young female, dressed in a pretty, but also very sexy, white lace mini dress and white heels entered the room. It suddenly occurred to me that the ladies from these sites had to dress with class and not look like a call girl when working in the hotels. I'm sure the hotels didn't allow it.

I watched as she slowly entered the room and looked over at Ricky, who was still looking out the window.

"Hello. I'm Carina," she said in a friendly voice.

As soon as she was well enough away from the door, I quickly slammed it shut and Ricky turned around and smiled.

"Hello Annie."

I couldn't see her face from where I stood, but from the satisfactory grin on Ricky's face, I'm certain it was a classic look of utter shock.

Her reply didn't match her classy attire. She spat out one word. "Fuck!" She immediately dashed for the door.

I quickly intervened and stood in front of the door with my arms blocking her escape. After seeing her face for the first time, I immediately saw the resemblance between her and Ricky. They had the same dark chestnut hair and high cheekbones. Her mouth narrowed just like Ricky's when he became frustrated. Annie was doing it now. I snapped at her as she raced towards the door and stood my ground. I spoke with a sharp tone. "Oh no you don't missy. You have some explaining to do and you are not leaving until you do." I didn't wait for her to reply. I wanted answers as much as Ricky, now that I had confirmation the woman was Annie. "Do you know that me and your brother are supposed to be on our honeymoon? And by the way, the wedding was beautiful. I'm sorry you couldn't make it, but I see now that you were busy."

Annie narrowed her eyes at me and snarled, "get out of my way, bitch. I don't have to talk to you."

I folded my arms and leaned back against the door. "Well, that's not a nice way to talk to your new sister-in-law."

Ricky marched across the room, grabbed Annie's arm, and spun her round. He gave her a hard stare and kept a firm grip on her. "What the hell is going on, Annie? What do you think you are doing?"

She tried to shake herself free, but failed. "I don't have to answer to you either, Ricky. Mind your own business, okay?"

"No, I won't. You are my sister and I want to know what the hell you are doing here in Vegas, working for an escort service?"

"I want to know, too," I butted in. "Ricky has been going crazy ever since he saw you in the elevator earlier today."

"Yes, Annie, I left you a message. Didn't you get it?"

Annie tried again to break free from Ricky by shaking her arm, but he refused to let her go.

"Talk to me Annie," Ricky hollered.

"Goddamnit Ricky. Yes, I got your message, okay? I was going to call you back in a couple of days."

"What? And deny it was you I saw and give yourself enough time to make up a believable story? "

Annie twisted her arm. "Will you let go of me? You are hurting my arm."

"Are you going to tell me what is going on?" Ricky persisted.

"Do I have a choice?"

"No!" I yelled, still blocking the door.

Ricky slowly released his hold on Annie and stepped away. I remained in front of the door with my arms folded. "We are waiting," I said impatiently.

Annie raised her hands in defeat, but I still expected her to make a dash for the door and held my ground by blocking it.

"Okay. Okay. Can I sit down? I need a cigarette," she said in a softer tone.

"When did you start smoking? This is a non-smoking room and you can't smoke in here," Ricky snapped.

"I've been smoking for years. You know nothing about me, Ricky." She scanned the room. "Why the hell did you get a non-smoking room?"

"Because we don't smoke. Duh," I called from my position at the door.

Annie took a seat on the edge of the bed. "So you are a married man now, eh, Ricky?"

"Quit changing the subject, Annie. Tell me how you ended up in Vegas. What happened to the jerk in Los Angeles? I can't remember his name."

"It's Adam, and I left him months ago."

Ricky creased his brow. "How many months ago, and why didn't you tell me or mom?"

Annie rubbed her brow and shook her head. "I don't know, maybe six months." She looked at Ricky with sad eyes. Her mood turned somber and tears trickled down her cheeks. I walked away from the door and stood beside Ricky, eager to hear what she would tell us next. Both Ricky and I remained silent to allow her to tell us her story.

"He beat me, Ricky. Sometimes so bad to where my body was covered in bruises. He also killed our baby. Last year I was pregnant and he beat me so bad I lost the baby."

Ricky and I gasped at the same time as we listened to Annie pour her heart out. My mood also switched. I suddenly felt sorry for her. The anger I had felt had completely gone and was replaced with pity. Shocked by what we were hearing, I took Ricky's hand and together we sat on the edge of the bed next to Annie and listened while she told us more.

"He was an alcoholic, and a mean one at that. He never worked." She released a sarcastic, painful laugh. "Shit, he couldn't hold down a job. He drank from morning till night and the more he drank, the worse he got. I was his punching bag Ricky, and for two and a half years I took it like a fool. Thinking I deserved every punch he gave me. But after I lost the baby, I started to fight back. For every punch he threw at me, I'd punch back. That was a mistake. It only released more fire in him and he'd hit me harder than the punch before."

Ricky finally spoke. His voice was soft. "Why didn't you call me or mom, or the cops?"

Annie shrugged her shoulders. "Too much pride, I guess. Ricky, I am almost thirty years old. I'm the eldest. I ain't running to my baby brother, or mom, and what would the cops do? Arrest him and keep him in jail for a night. They wouldn't be there when I returned home to face the consequences. He'd be furious because I had him arrested. He would have been in such a rage that he would have probably killed me."

"Did he drink when you first met him?" I asked.

"He did, like we all did at parties and stuff, but gradually he drank more, until he turned into a monster that I no longer knew. The day I left, he beat me again right before I left to go to work. It was in the afternoon, and he was pissed because he was out of vodka, and told me to bring him a bottle home on my way back from work. Sadly, I made the mistake of telling him I had barely enough money to pay the light bill, which was going to be shut off any day. I was already two months behind. I told him I couldn't afford to buy his booze. Well, that's where I fucked up. He pushed me into a corner and just started hitting me. I covered my face with my hands, but my legs and stomach were all bruised up. After work that night, I just kept driving. I couldn't go back, and I ended up here in Vegas."

There was silence in the room. I was still trying to digest the horrific story Annie had just confided in us. She uncrossed and recrossed her legs and shifted her body on the bed.

"Now, if you give me a beer, I'll tell you the rest of the story and how I ended up doing what I'm doing."

CHAPTER 14

*R*icky was the first one to jump off the bed and grab a beer from the bar. I remained sitting next to Annie and gave her a sympathetic smile. I still didn't know what to say. How does one respond to what she had just told us? I've heard about women being beaten and struggling to survive, but I've never met someone in person who was actually living the nightmare.

My perspective on Annie had changed. I had such admiration for her courage, and I wanted to reach out and hold her. But I feared she would push me away after the way I had spoken to her when she had first entered the room. I realized then how lucky I had been throughout my life. My complaints and acts of selflessness seemed so minuscule compared to what Annie had been and was still going through. I'll think twice before I complain about anything again.

My mother was my biggest complaint, but I have to admit, she gave me a good life, and it was all she knew, and fitted in with her lifestyle. She lacked communication skills and compassion, but so did I, for most of my life, until Travis had his accident, which turned me around and made me change my ways. Maybe speaking the truth and standing up to my mom for the first time enlightened her? Maybe there is still some hope for us and our severed relationship.

Ricky returned to the edge of the bed with three opened bottles of Budweiser. I quickly grabbed one and took a large gulp, while Ricky returned to his place. "So tell us how you ended up working for an escort service?" Ricky asked.

Annie took a deep breath and a long swig of her beer before telling us more. "Well, it wasn't planned." She cracked a sarcastic laugh. "Shit, no one plans to work for an escort service. All the girls I know were down on their luck and desperate, just like me. When I arrived in Vegas in the early hours of the morning, I was a mess. I could barely focus on the last few miles of driving. I had cried for most of the drive and was exhausted. Most of my tips had gone for gas, a stale sandwich, and a cup of cold coffee from a gas station. I had no place to go, and no idea what I was going to do. The only thing that felt good was that I was miles away from Adam and he couldn't hurt me anymore. I left with nothing but the clothes on my back, and my phone, which I still have by the way, but the people I work for have no idea I have it. It's the only thing I have that connects me to you and mom."

"Yeah, mom told me she pays the bill."

Annie nodded. "Yes, she does. I'll explain why soon." She shifted again and took another swig of beer before telling us more. "I pulled into a coffee shop and used the last of my money to buy a decent cup of coffee and a donut. I don't know how long I sat there, looking out the window, wondering what I was going to do next. But sometime later, a middle-aged, well-dressed man approached me and took a seat at my table across from me. He was super friendly and knew all the right things to say. After I had spilled my guts out to him, I confessed I had no money, and I was a homeless lost soul. He reached out and took my hand. He told me he had a house where I could stay with five other girls. All my bills, rent, and food would be taken care of. I was desperate, and he knew it. I ended up following him to the house, where he introduced me to Savanna. She is the head of the household and takes care of all the girls' needs. She buys our clothes, food and cosmetics. Well, Savanna was just as good as the guy in the restaurant when it came to words. She took me in her arms, held me tight, and told me exactly what I wanted to hear, that they were going to take me in, and everything was going to be okay. The other girls joined in and told me how much they loved living in the house. They felt safe and were surrounded by friends. By now, I just wanted a place to lay my head, and that's exactly what they allowed me to do. Savannah led me to a cute little room with a bed, and told me to sleep as long as I needed to. I slept for two days, and when I walked into the kitchen, Savanna and all the girls, sitting at the table drinking coffee and eating a home-cooked breakfast, greeted me. They all looked so happy and I wanted to be happy, just like they were. After Savanna filled my belly with bacon and eggs, she took me into the office and told me that the girls stayed at the house for free and in return they entertained some men friends. I knew what she meant, but didn't want to come out and say it in case I insulted her. I had nowhere to go and figured I could do it for a month or so until I got back on my feet."

"So what happened? Why are you still there?" Ricky asked.

"Because I don't get any money, Ricky. How am I supposed to save enough to make it on my own when we don't get any cash? Our form of payment is room and board, food and whatever else we may need. Savanna makes sure we have everything we need. Which is why I let mom pay for my cell phone. The one I have for work, Savanna pays."

"So you are stuck?" Ricky said.

Annie nodded. "Yes, I am, until I figure out how the hell I can get out of that place."

Ricky stood and began pacing the room. Deep in thought, he tapped his head for ideas. After a few minutes, he stopped and gave Annie a hard stare. "You are not going back there. I can't let you."

Annie quickly stood and placed her hands on her hips. She snarled at Ricky. His words triggered her. "Don't you dare tell me what to do. Adam controlled me, and I won't let you control me."

Ricky couldn't hide the shock of Annie's sudden outburst. "I'm just looking out for you. It's what families do, Annie. Jesus, you have a degree in journalism. What the hell are you doing? How do you think mom is going to react to this?"

Annie's nostrils flared when she yelled. "Don't you dare tell mom! This is none of her business, nor yours for that matter."

Ricky stopped pacing and glared at Annie. "Well, I'm making it my business. You think I'm just going to return to San Diego like everything is normal, knowing what you are doing here? I can't Annie, I'm sorry."

"You are going to have to, Ricky. This is my life, and you can't tell me what to do just because you don't agree with it. I'll get my life back together. Don't you worry, and trust me, you will be the first to know."

I had no words of advice. It was clear Annie wouldn't accept any help from us. It seemed stubbornness ran in the family. I've seen Ricky act the same way often, even when we first started dating. I was the one that seduced him because he refused to give me another chance. There was an uncomfortable silence in the room, and I made an excuse to leave. "Hey, I have to use the bathroom. I'll be right back." Neither Ricky nor Annie acknowledged my announcement as I stood from the bed and exited the room, closing the bathroom door quickly behind me. I heard Ricky start up the conversation again.

"I need to think, Annie. I'm not okay with this."

"Think all you want, Ricky. It ain't going to change anything. This is my life, not yours. You have no say."

From the bathroom, I heard footsteps. They were heavy, and I assumed it was Ricky pacing the room like he normally did when he was deep in thought. Again there was silence, and I went to pee.

While in the middle of my task, I suddenly heard Ricky yell from the other room.

"Annie! Come back here."

I heard Ricky run across the room towards the door that led out to the hallway. He yelled again, "Annie!"

"What the fuck?" I said out loud, rushing my business and quickly pulling up my panties, before racing to the door. "What the hell is going on?" I hollered, as I returned to what was now an empty room. I scanned the area. There was no one with me. "Ricky!" I yelled, as I raced to the open door and looked in both directions of the hallway. It was empty. "What the hell just happened?" I asked myself, as I marched down the corridor to the elevator that was now descending, wondering if Ricky and Annie were inside, duking it out. I had no choice but to return to the room and wait for Ricky's and, hopefully, Annie's return.

CHAPTER 15

Unable to relax, confused by what had just happened, I left the door open and listened intently for footsteps coming down the hallway. Why did Annie bolt? How could she go back to the life she was living? I'm not sure how much time passed, but I suddenly heard heavy footsteps coming down the hallway. I dashed to the doorway and saw Ricky stomping towards our room. His chest was heaving, and I allowed him to catch his breath before he spoke.

After he entered the room, I looked down the hallway, "where's Annie?" I said, as I closed the door.

"She's gone. I tried to chase after her, but these damn hallways are like friggin' mazes. I have no idea which one she took." Ricky took a seat on the edge of the bed and raked his hands through his hair. "I was staring out the window, trying to think how we could help her. She must have snuck over to the door, and it wasn't until I heard someone running down the hallway that I turned around and saw the door wide open and that she was gone."

I took a seat next to him and rested my hand on his knees. It crushed me to see him so distraught. "I guess there is nothing we can do. We could have helped her if she had stayed."

Ricky pushed my hand aside and stood. "We have to find her. I can't leave here until we do."

I raised my voice, "Ricky, may I remind you we are supposed to be on our honeymoon? Annie chose to leave. There is nothing more we can do for her."

Ricky shook his head and marched across the room. "Screw the honeymoon, Jill. We are talking about my sister here. You can't expect me to spend the rest of the week here and not think about Annie and what she is doing. I'm sorry, but I can't do it."

It was at that moment that I knew the honeymoon was over. "So, how do you plan on finding her?"

"I don't know yet. I need some time to think."

I scanned the room, and a terrible thought came over me. "Hey where is my purse?" I looked at the small table, where I was certain I had left it, and then looked at the bed. "It's not here," I gasped. Racing to the side of the bed, I checked under it. My heart raced as I stood and quickly checked the room again. "Ricky, my purse is gone," I said in a panicked state.

Ricky quickly stood and began searching the few surfaces in the room. "What? Are you sure?"

I checked and rechecked the table, the bed, and the nightstand. "Yes, I'm positive. It's not here."

"What about the bathroom?" Ricky hollered from the floor, where he had kneeled to look under the bed again.

I marched to the bathroom. "I'll check," I snapped, before turning on the lights and scanning the counter. "No, it's not in here. That bitch stole my purse," I screamed. "It still had the $5,000 I won."

Ricky's jaw dropped, and his eyes grew wide. "What!"

I raised my hands in despair. "Yes, it was still in my purse. I hadn't put it in the safe yet. So much has been going on that it slipped my mind."

"God damn it. Now we really need to find her. I can't believe she stole from us."

"It's not only the money, Ricky. She has my ID and my credit cards. Do you know what a headache it's going to be to replace all that shit?" I flopped my body on the bed and let my head fall into the pillow. "I don't believe this shit."

Ricky sat on the edge of the bed next to me and buried his head in his palms. "Why did she have to steal from us? We told her we would help her."

"I don't know Ricky. All I know is that we are out $5,000 and I have no ID. How am I supposed to get on the plane when we leave this awful place? God, what a mess this is."

"Are you sure you couldn't have left it somewhere else? Like the pool or the bar?"

I shook my head. "No, I had it with me when we were at the bar talking to that guy. I took my phone out of it to write down the website. Remember?"

"Oh, yeah, that's right." Ricky raked his hair with his fingers. "Shit, not only does Annie work for an escort service, but she is also a thief."

We sat in silence on the bed. My head was spinning with the headache I now faced with replacing my ID and credit cards. This couldn't be happening.

The white room phone on the nightstand rang, startling both of us. "Who could that be?" Ricky said with a creased brow, as he walked over to the nightstand and answered the phone. "Hello?"

Unable to hear the voice on the other end of the line, I questioned who it was too.

I saw Ricky's eyes light up as he listened to the voice on the line. "Really. Thank you. We will be right down," Ricky said with a smile. I waited until he had hung up.

"Who was that?" I asked, puzzled by his sudden change of mood.

"That was the front desk. Someone handed in your purse."

"What? That makes no sense. I know it was here in this room. Is everything in it?"

"They didn't say. Come on. We can ask who turned it in when we pick it up."

When we reached the front desk, a friendly young man greeted us. Ricky quickly made his case. "Someone called and said my wife's purse had been handed in."

The man smiled. "Let me see what I can find out. I will be right back."

Ricky and I anxiously waited hand-in-hand, as we watched him talk to other staff members. I saw a female co-worker nod, and they disappeared together through a door at the end of the desk. A few minutes later, he returned with my purse in his hands.

He held it up. "Is this it?" he asked with a friendly smile.

I shrieked, "yes!" as I grabbed it from his hands. "Thank you," and hastily pulled out my wallet.

"Do you know who turned it in?" Ricky asked, as I fumbled to open my wallet.

He pointed to his co-worker. "Sharon told me a young woman wearing a white dress turned it in about ten minutes ago. You are very lucky."

I looked up. "What? That was Annie. She stole my purse and then returned it. That doesn't make any sense."

The man behind the desk left to help other customers, leaving us alone. "Is everything there?" Ricky asked.

"Hold on. Let me check." My heart sank when I unzipped my wallet. "No, all the money's gone. She took all the cash, Ricky."

"And left your ID and credit cards. That's weird."

"Hold on, there's a piece of paper." I pulled it out and read the note out loud. "I'm sorry. I'll pay you back." My jaw dropped in disbelief. "What the fuck? How the hell is she going to pay us back?" I hissed.

Ricky grabbed the note from my hand and studied it. "Unbelievable. My own sister stole from us. Why?" He released a sarcastic laugh. "Well, at least she returned your ID and credit cards, saving us the hassle of canceling them and getting new ones."

"I'm not giving her any slack, Ricky," I snapped, as I snatched the note from his hand. "She stole my purse and took $5,000. I don't care that she returned the rest. She is a thief, and I also don't care that she is your sister. I'll never trust her."

My blood was boiling. I've never had anything stolen, and to make it worse, it was someone I knew and was supposed to be family. It enraged me. Does she have no morals? How could I ever trust her again, or forgive her for doing this to us? Not only did she steal from us, but she also ruined our honeymoon. I'll be damned if I'm going to spend the rest of it searching for her. The honeymoon was over and I was ready to pack our things and go home. With disgust, I shoved the note and wallet in my purse. "Come on, let's go back to our room. I'm done here," I snapped, as I stormed off towards the elevator.

The elevator was crowded, and we didn't speak until we entered our room. I threw my purse on the bed and stared at Ricky with my arms folded. "I've had enough of this place and I want to go home."

Ricky grabbed a beer from the wet bar and popped off the cap with force. He took a large swig. "We are not going home, Jill. I'm going to find Annie, and she is coming home with us."

I yelled across the room. "I don't want that woman anywhere near me. Ricky, and I sure as hell want nothing to do with her. How can you even think about saving her? She chose her life and now we are out $5,000 because of it."

Ricky gave me a stare and waved his hands in the air. "Then go home Jill, but I'm not. I told you, I'm not leaving here without her. I have to find her. I'm sorry, but I mean it."

His words stunned me. He was serious. His eyes couldn't hide the pain he was feeling. "You are serious, aren't you? You would let me go home alone?"

Ricky nodded. "Yes, I would. Nothing is going to happen to you if you go home. You will be surrounded by friends, and Maggie will be there to protect you, but something might happen to Annie. I know nothing about the people she works for. How do you expect me to leave and not worry about her and her safety?"

I sat on the edge of the bed, realizing I wasn't going to be able to convince Ricky to leave, and in my heart I knew I could never leave without him. He was my husband, and Annie was his sister. To abandon him would be wrong. I looked across the room. "Okay then. So, how are we going to find her?"

Ricky gave me a puzzled look. "You mean you will stay?"

I nodded and gave him a weak smile. "Yes, I will stay."

Ricky raced across the room and held out his arms to embrace me.

I quickly raised my hands. "I'm only staying because you are my husband, and it's the right thing to do, and because she is your sister."

CHAPTER 16

Ricky approached me and wrapped me in his arms. He gave me a gentle kiss on the lips. "Thank you for staying."

"Yeah, like I said, I'm doing this for you, not her." I rested my hands on his shoulders. "So, what do we do now?"

"I don't know. I have to think." He pulled out his phone from his back pocket. "The first thing I'm going to do is to send her a long message, letting her know exactly what I think of her and that it's not safe for her to be here alone. I'm also going to ask her again to please come home with us."

I pulled away from his embrace to give him space to use his phone. "Do you honestly think she will reply?"

Ricky sat at the small round table and began texting. "She probably won't, but at least she will know how I feel. Maybe she will change her mind and leave with us."

I left Ricky to finish texting, and decided to check in on Sadie to see how Maggie was doing. I was missing her more with each passing hour. Being away from her, I realized how much comfort she gave me. I chuckled at the thought that I was probably missing her more than she was missing me. I love how she nuzzles her snout under my chin and wags her tail while I bury my head in her coat of fur. I could use one of those special doggie moments right about now.

Sadie texted me back immediately, along with an adorable picture of Maggie holding one of her favorite stuffed toys. "Aww, I miss our girl." I held up my phone, turning the screen to face Ricky. "Look, she sent me a picture of Maggie."

Ricky looked up and smiled. "I miss her too," and then returned to texting. A few minutes later, he released a heavy sigh and put down his phone. "There, done, and I held nothing back."

"As you shouldn't. What she did was just wrong, and especially to family. I have no idea how we are going to find her. She'll probably never come back to this hotel. Well, at least while we are staying here."

Ricky left the table and joined me on the bed. "You are right. For all we know, she may have taken that money and left Vegas already."

"And where would she go?" I questioned.

"I don't know. But why else would she take the money, unless she saw it as her way to escape and start a new life somewhere? She left Los Angeles on a whim with nothing. What's stopping her from doing the same here?"

"You got a point. So we could spend the rest of our honeymoon looking for her, and she may not even be here."

"I hope that's not the case. I need answers, and I will stay here for as long as it takes."

I sat up from my relaxed position. "Ricky, we can't stay here indefinitely. We have a life back in San Diego, and may I remind you, jobs and Maggie. If we haven't found her by the time our honeymoon is up, I'm sorry, but we have to go home."

Ricky looked at me and spoke with a serious tone that had me concerned. "I'm sorry Jill, I don't know if I can."

I raised my hand to my brow and gave it a vigorous rub. "My god Ricky, I can't stay past our honeymoon. I'll get fired. Slater will find someone else too. He only has you covered until the end of the week. We have to get back to our lives. You are seriously considering throwing it all in for Annie, who may I remind you, just stole $5,000 from us. Why?"

"You know why. She's my sister. How many times do I have to say it?"

I stood up off the bed and continued to rub my forehead as I paced the room, trying to reason with Ricky. "Is that the only reason? You haven't seen her in years, and now suddenly you want to be a hero and rescue her from a life that she has chosen for herself, by the way."

"She wasn't an escort in Los Angeles, and I'm afraid for her safety. Nothing good can come of it, Jill. She is bound to run into some sort of trouble, eventually."

"How do we know that, Ricky? And we can't force her to just up and leave because we want her to. She is an adult. You are not her guardian, Ricky." I raised my voice a notch. "God, I wish I could talk some sense into you."

My words annoyed Ricky. "Jill, I wish you would stop giving me a hard time about this. A few minutes ago, you said you would stay here with me."

"Yes, until our honeymoon is over. But we can't stay a day over. I'm not going to lose my job over this, and you can't either."

Ricky stormed off the bed and grabbed his jacket from the back of the chair. "I need some time to think. I'm going for a walk. Don't wait up for me."

I gasped, "what? You're leaving?" I grabbed his shoulder as he pulled his arm through the sleeve of his jacket.

He jerked his shoulder away from my hand and finished putting on his jacket. "Just for a little while. I need some air."

"But we need to talk about this. How do you plan on looking for her?"

Ricky grabbed his phone and shoved it in the back of his jeans. "I don't know, Jill. All of your questions are driving me nuts." He stormed over to the door and opened it with force. "I'll be back," he said in a sharp tone, before leaving the room and slamming the door.

CHAPTER 17

The sudden silence in the room was painful. Tears pooled in my eyes. How could he leave me alone on our honeymoon? I wanted nothing more than to leave and forget about this entire trip. We haven't even been married for a week, and he doesn't even want to talk to me. He wants to be alone. Is this how our marriage is going to be? Ricky takes the easy way out by leaving instead of talking to me?

This is all Annie's fault. God, I hate that bitch. I don't care if she is Ricky's sister. Look at what she is doing to my marriage. If we ever find her, I'm going to tell her exactly what I think of her. Ricky has another thing coming if he thinks she is coming home with us. He is asking a little too much from me to allow that to happen.

I noticed my phone laying on the bed and flopped my body next to it before I picked it up and glanced at the screen. My heart sank when I saw I had no messages or voicemails. I really needed to talk to someone and stared at the screen, contemplating calling Sabela, but quickly decided against it. I didn't want to drown her with my problems. She had enough going on with taking care of Slater and the kids, and besides, I wanted her to believe we were having a fantastic time. It occurred to me at that moment that I wasn't sure if I'd ever tell her about this rotten honeymoon we were having.

An hour passed with no phone call or message from Ricky. My mood shifted from being upset to angry. How dare he treat me this way and shut me out? Why the hell didn't he stay and talk to me? Together, we could have figured something out. I'm in this as much as he is. I jumped off the bed, and screamed at the dead air in the room, "I'm your wife! God damn it, Ricky!" I ripped off my clothes and threw them across the room, and passed on washing my face or cleaning my teeth. Instead, I climbed into bed and yanked the sheets up to my chin.

Another half-hour passed, and my anger was still elevated. I found it impossible to sleep, not knowing the whereabouts of Ricky. Footsteps in the hallway caught my attention, and I pinned my ears, and then heard movement on the other side of the door. Ricky was using his key card and soon entered the room.

He looked my way with a blank stare. "Hey," he said, as he flopped into the chair by the table.

I sat up and folded my arms. "Hey, that's all you have to say? Where have you been?"

Ricky leaned back in the chair and rubbed his face with his palms. "Jill, don't give me a hard time. I told you I had to think."

I wasn't going to let him off that easily. "Well, are you going to share your thoughts with me? I am your wife, you know."

Ricky released a heavy sigh and closed his eyes. "Can we talk about this in the morning? I'm exhausted."

I stormed off the bed and approached him with my hands on my hips. "No Ricky, I want to talk about this now. You have been gone for almost two hours. We are supposed to be on our honeymoon, and this is not how I imagined it."

"Me neither Jill. I didn't exactly plan this. What do you want me to do?"

My anger subsided a little. He had asked me for advice. He was finally letting me in. "I want us to work together and try to figure out a way to find Annie. Don't shut me out, Ricky. I'm your wife, and we are supposed to be partners." He caressed my hand with his and I rested my hand on his shoulder. I gave it a squeeze. "I'm on your side, Ricky, but when you take off and exclude me, I take offense."

He looked at me with sad eyes, looking so lost. "I don't know what to do, Jill."

I leaned in, and Ricky embraced my middle, where I stood before him. As I listened to him, I buried my face in his hair. "I love you, Ricky. We will find her," I said in a soothing tone as I stroked his hair. "Come on. Let's crawl into bed," I suggested, as I took his hand.

Once under the cool sheets, Ricky cradled me in his arms. I breathed in his scent, and snuggled my naked body close to his, and rested my head on his bare chest. I smiled when he kissed the top of my head and pulled me in closer.

"I'm sorry I took off. There is so much going on in my head over this. I just don't know what to do."

I patted his chest. "It's okay. Try to get some sleep. We will wake up with fresh minds and figure out what to do."

Silence came between us as we tried to drift off to sleep. After what seemed a long time, I spoke again. "Are you awake?"

"Yes," Ricky replied, without an essence of fatigue.

I sat up and turned on the lamp next to the bed. "I can't sleep either."

Ricky followed suit and sat up next to me. "Me neither. What time is it?"

I picked up my phone and glanced at the screen. "Almost 3:00 AM."

"I wonder if Annie is with some other dude right now?"

"Ricky don't. Let's not think about it."

"That's all I'm thinking about. It's why I can't sleep. Isn't that why you can't?"

I shrugged my shoulders. "Well, yeah, but not because I'm wondering if she is with some guy. I've been lying here racking my brain, trying to think of a way to find her so we can get past all this and move on."

"Have you come up with anything?"

"Well, I'm not sure, because, like we said, she may have taken the money and split. But if she is still at that place, I may have an idea that might work."

Ricky's eyes grew wide. "Well, tell me."

I positioned my body in a more comfortable position and leaned back against the headboard. "Well, if she's still working for the same service, we could book her again from the website."

Ricky creased his brow. "That won't work, Jill. She won't come back here. We've already assumed that."

"Hear me out, okay? What if we have her come to another hotel?"

"I'm not following you?"

I rolled my eyes. "We can get a room at another hotel and have her meet us there."

Ricky gave it some thought before he spoke. "That might just work, but we can't use my name and credit card again. Her boss, or whoever takes the bookings, might tell her I'm a repeat customer. She may put two and two together. I'm not even sure if they discuss those kinds of details with her, but I don't want to take any chances."

I nodded, "good point." I thought for a moment. "Well, I have a credit card and we can open a new account with that one."

"But you're a woman."

I chuckled at his observation. "Yes, I am, and I'm sure the girls in escort services go both ways."

Ricky scrunched his face. "Even Annie?"

"Yes, even Annie."

Ricky fell back into the pillows. "Wow, I never thought of that. What a vision." He shook his head. "I can't have those thoughts."

"So, do you want to try it?"

Ricky raised his hands. "Well, what do we have to lose? It's our only option."

"Great. Tomorrow we will check to see if she is still on the website. If she is, we will book a room at another hotel, and have her meet us there tomorrow night."

Ricky nodded and forced a smile. "This may just work."

"Only if she is still with the website. If she is not, then we are back to square one."

CHAPTER 18

$\mathcal{B}$ecause of our lack of sleep, Ricky and I slept in until almost eleven. I woke up wrapped in his arms, and was greeted by his warm smile and a soft sensual kiss on the lips.

"Good morning, sleeping beauty," he said, as he slipped his arm from around my neck.

I returned the smile, and blinked a few times. "Hey, you seem like you're in a better mood."

Ricky pulled the sheets back and stood before me, naked. He reached for a pair of shorts and I admired the view. "I am," he smiled. "I'm anxious to get some food inside of us, and then check out the website."

I laughed at his enthusiasm. "Okay, let me get dressed. I'm starving too."

After filling our bellies with omelets, toast, and coffee, we both took some time to check our phones, and I immediately hissed when I saw I had another text from my mom. "Crap," I moaned out loud.

"What's wrong?" Ricky asked, while not taking his eyes off his screen.

I placed my phone facedown on the table and leaned back in the booth. "My mom texted me again."

"Are you going to text her back?"

I folded my arms, and answered with no hesitation, "no."

Ricky put down his phone and gave me a puzzled look. "It sounds like she wants to make amends. What did she say?"

"Not much. She asked if I got her last text and to text her back. No apology, no nothing." I rolled my eyes. "She can wait. I'm not going to let her have the satisfaction of ruining my honeymoon. Annie has already done that."

Ricky reached across the table and took my hand. "I'm really sorry, Jill. I'll make it up to you after this is all behind us."

"Oh, I know you will. You owe me big time," I joked, before returning my phone to my purse. "Come on, let's get out of here. We have some detective work to do."

When we returned to our room, we didn't start our mission straight away. After our horrible night last night, we both had an urge to connect. Ricky wasted no time. Once the door was closed, he took me in his arms and kissed me tenderly, as he slowly peeled off my clothes. I didn't resist. I wanted him to seduce me, and take me. I began to undress him as I stood before him, naked. There were no words needed between us. Our emotions and lust spoke for the two of us. We devoured each other and caressed every inch of each other's bodies, raising our temperatures a few degrees. Our kisses were passionate, and the love making was fierce. We were on fire, and our bodies trembled with explosive orgasms as we reached them together.

Our chests heaved as our heads fell back into the pillows with our skin drenched in sweat. "Wow," I gasped, as I tried to catch my breath.

Ricky breathed heavily next to me. His hand rested on his brow, and his eyes were closed. His lungs continued to suck in air, and his pants were short and quick, "damn woman, you are going to be the death of me."

I giggled, and snuggled next to him, as my breathing returned to normal, "that was fantastic." I bounced in bed. "Now this is how a honeymoon should be."

Ricky sat up and swung his legs over the edge of the bed. "As much as I want to lie here next to you, we need to look into finding Annie."

I frowned and released a groan. "I know. Give me a minute to put on my bathrobe and brush my hair."

When I returned from the bathroom, Ricky had also put on the hotel's white bathrobe, and was sitting up on the bed browsing his phone. I grabbed my phone from the end table and crawled onto the bed next to him. "Have you found anything?" I asked.

"No, not yet. I just typed in the website, and I'm trying to log in. He looked my way. "What's my password?"

"Here, give me your phone," I said, as I took it and punched in his password. I immediately scrolled and found Annie under recommendations. "There she is," I squealed.

Ricky quickly took my phone to take a closer look. "So, she is still working for them?"

"That, or the website hasn't been updated yet."

"Open up an account and try to book her. See if it will let you," Ricky suggested.

I immediately went to work and began tapping on my phone. After fifteen minutes, I had an account under the user's name of Desiree using my credit card. "I'm in," I said with pride.

"Great, now see if you can book her."

"Okay. Give me a minute." I gave him a puzzled look. "I can't book her until we have a room somewhere else."

"Shit, you are right. Give me a second."

I waited while Ricky searched hotels, and after a few minutes, he smiled, "Okay, I got us a room at the Bellagio."

I released a heavy sigh. "Shoot."

"What's wrong?" Ricky asked, as he glanced at my phone.

"Earliest time is 8:00 PM tomorrow night."

Ricky took my phone. "What?" How many dudes does she see a day?"

"Maybe she is off today. We don't know."

"Yeah, maybe. Okay, I'll change the reservations at the other hotel for tomorrow night."

Ricky said, while tapping on his phone.

I nodded and clicked *confirm* on my phone. "Okay, we're all set for 8 o'clock tomorrow night. I wonder how this will all go down?"

"Guess we will find out tomorrow night," Ricky said. "But in the meantime, we get to spend some quality time together." He reached over and tickled me, before rolling his body onto mine. "What do you want to do?"

"Play the slots and go walk the strip with you?" I said with a huge grin.

"You got it," he said with a smile, and slapped my behind before leaving the bed. "Get dressed. I am all yours for the next eighteen hours."

CHAPTER 19

For the next day and a half, Ricky and I acted like newlyweds. We did not discuss Annie. When I caught Ricky at times, in deep thought, I suspected he was thinking about her and didn't want to ruin our precious time together by bringing up her name, so I let him be in his thoughts alone. On those occasions, I made the excuse to use the restroom, play the slots if they were close by, which they always are in Vegas, or buy a snack. Even though Ricky was still troubled by Annie's doings, as was I, I appreciated him not letting it dampen our time together. There will be plenty of time tomorrow when we confront her for a second time.

During our time, we squeezed in a couple of shows, had lunch at the Hard Rock Cafe, and cocktails at a few lounges while playing in the casinos. Ricky's mood remained positive most of the time, but when we arrived at the Bellagio Hotel to check into our room, his mood shifted. His smile disappeared, and he seemed unsettled while standing in line at the front desk. I rested my hand on his shoulder. "Hey, are you okay?"

"Yeah, I'll just be glad when this is all over."

"How do you see it ending?" I asked.

Ricky looked surprised by my question. "Well, she's coming home with us. I thought I had made that perfectly clear."

"And if she doesn't want to?"

Ricky pulled away from my hand and folded his arms. "She doesn't have a choice, Jill."

"Ricky, we can't force her."

Ricky approached the desk and gave his name to the pretty blonde, who immediately began typing on the computer keyboard. "When the time comes," he said, "we will discuss this." He grabbed the key card from the receptionist and slid it into his back pocket. He scanned the area. "Wanna get a drink?"

"Sure."

After we settled in the bar drinking our cocktails, I found myself checking out the older men with younger females hooked on their arms. I wondered how many were hired through an escort service, like the one Annie worked for. I didn't share my thoughts with Ricky, who was busy texting Slater on his phone. After he was finished, I spoke.

"How's Slater doing?"

"Much better. He's back on the job, but not doing any heavy lifting. Sabela says hi, and they've invited us over for dinner when we get back."

"Awesome. I miss those babies. Being an aunt is something I love. I should buy them something from Vegas. An outfit or something."

Ricky nodded. "They have stores here at the hotel. Do you want to go check them out? I'm not sure when we will have time again after tonight."

I took a large sip of my margarita. "Good idea. I want to buy a wig too. I'm sure they have some here because I've seen them in other stores in the hotels."

Ricky creased his brow. "A wig? Why are you planning on doing some role playing in the bedroom or something?" he joked.

I laughed, "no, but that's not a bad idea. I was thinking about our setup with Annie. How are we going to play this out? She is expecting to see a woman when she comes to our room. Well, I need to be in disguise so she doesn't immediately try to run again, don't you think?"

Ricky leaned back in his chair and raised his finger up to his chin. "I never thought about that. And what about me? I'll have to be hiding in the room somewhere."

I leaned forward and smiled. "I've given this some thought while we've been out and about. I thought about wearing a long black wig, a lot more makeup and heavy red lipstick, which is something I would never wear, and maybe talk with a French accent. I want to make sure she doesn't recognize me."

"I like it, and what about me?"

"Well, I think you should hide in the bathroom, but behind the shower curtains and leave the door open a little. Otherwise, she may think someone is in there if the door is closed."

"Good point." Ricky sat up and smiled. "You have given this some thought. Thanks."

I grinned, "you're welcome. Now come on. We have some shopping to do."

An hour later we were in our room, and after scoping out the bathroom, I was pleased to see they had shower curtains and not glass doors. I tossed my shopping bags on the bed, and Ricky placed our small luggage bag on a chair near the table. We only brought a change of clothes and my makeup. I glanced at the clock on the end table. "We have a few hours before she arrives," I told Ricky. "Which gives us plenty of time to get ready and finalize our plan," I added.

Ricky was checking out the mini bar while I was speaking, and didn't answer me. "Ricky, did you hear me?"

"Yeah, I heard you. Do you want a beer?"

"Yeah, I need some liquid courage," I laughed.

Ricky came and sat on the edge of the bed, and handed me a

drink. I took a large swig. "So, how are we going to play this out? What am I supposed to say to her when she enters the room? I need to stall her, but not have sex with her," I laughed. "We need to have her in the room with the door closed. She has to be comfortable with the surroundings, and not suspect anything."

Ricky shrugged his shoulders. "I don't know. You're a woman. Strike up a conversation with her. What do women talk about?" Ricky asked.

"Men," I laughed. "Maybe I'll comment on her outfit. Ask her where she got it. Women love compliments. Especially when it's about their wardrobe. At some point, you need to come out of the bathroom. You're not leaving this all up to me, are you?"

"Of course not. Come up with a code or something, so I know when it's time to enter."

I thought for a moment. "I know. I'll make an excuse to close the bathroom door. When I'm at the door, instead of closing it, I'll push it open and you come out and do whatever you plan on doing?" I creased my brow. "What do you plan on doing, by the way?"

"Brilliant idea. I love it. As far as what am I going to do? I have no idea yet. I guess I will find out when the time comes."

I glanced at the clock again. "Okay, the clock is ticking. I need to get changed and then it's showtime baby," I said, as I grabbed the bag with the wig.

CHAPTER 20

I tried to stay positive while getting changed and manage the anger that I still felt towards Annie. I was doing this for Ricky, not for her. What he was going through tore at my heart. He tried so hard to not show his pain, but his eyes couldn't lie. He was hurting, and I knew he was worried about Annie. I had to force myself not to think about her stealing from us, and lying to us about why she didn't attend our wedding. If I did, my anger would kick in.

Dressed in a royal blue mini dress, and long black boots, I looked at myself in the mirror and was pleased with the results. I didn't recognize myself. The long black wig was full and thick, and covered a lot of my face with the long bangs, which took some getting used to. I had done my eyes with a heavy blue eyeshadow to match my dress, and found some fake eyelashes at the wig store. I actually loved the way they looked. They really made my eyes pop. After applying a thick coat of deep red lipstick, I whispered my alias name in a French accent, "Hello Desiree," and blew my reflection a kiss. "Are you ready to play?" I said in a sultry voice, enjoying my disguise.

I made a slow entrance to the bedroom, where I found Ricky buttoning his black shirt. With my hands on my hips, I cat walked over to him. He looked up and his eyes grew wide. "Wow! You look friggin' hot. I love the wig."

"I'd kiss you, but I don't want to ruin my lipstick," I joked.

Ricky took me in his arms. "Don't throw away the wig, okay? We will use it later," he said, followed by a wink and a kiss on my cheek.

I brought my finger up to my pursed lips. "Ooh sweetie, you want to have your way with Desiree?"

"You bet I do. If we didn't have plans, I'd be throwing you on that bed right now."

I giggled and spun around before giving him a light kiss on the lips. "There's a little taste."

Ricky slapped my behind. "This is so damn sexy. I can't wait until we are alone for an entire night, because when we are, watch out." He pulled away, grabbing his shoes and taking a seat to put them on.

I checked the time. "She should be here in half an hour. Let's go over our plan again," I suggested.

We conversed for the next twenty minutes, making sure we were on the same page. Ricky still had no idea what he was going to say to Annie, even though I tried to push him to come up with some kind of plan, but he refused.

"I'll know when I'm face to face with her. My emotions will tell me what to say. This isn't easy for me, Jill." He released a heavy sigh, "I wish we weren't doing this. I hate setting up my sister, but what choice do we have?"

"I understand what you are saying. It makes sense, and I'm sorry this is happening." I left the table where we sat and straightened my wig. "Okay, you need to go hide. She's going to be here any minute and I need to get into character."

Once Ricky was in the bathroom, I checked to make sure he had left the door open a little. He had. This time, I would answer the main door to our room when Annie knocked, unlike the last time when we had left it open. Left in the room alone, I took a deep breath and gathered my thoughts. I wondered how this was going to end? We needed to convince her somehow not to run away, but to stay with us and let us help her. I was having doubts and was unsure if we could pull it off.

A knock at the door distracted my thoughts, and I took another deep breath. "She's here," I whispered, as I passed the bathroom door.

Ricky whispered back. "Okay."

I paused before opening the door and quickly scanned the room to make sure nothing was left out that could give us a way. I didn't see anything and slowly opened the door, and found myself face to face with Annie. It took all my willpower not to slug her for what she had done. She was dressed in a yellow and white mini cocktail dress and white heeled sandals. I was amused that she was also wearing a blonde wig. It occurred to me at that moment that she probably changed her appearance often so as not to be detected by the hotel.

"Hello, I am Carina. Are you Desiree?" she said with a friendly smile.

I switched on my French accent and replied with a nod, as I opened the door wider to welcome her in. "Oui. Please, won't you come in?"

My chest was pounding as she entered the room, and I rubbed my sweaty palms as I watched her stand in the middle of the room and glance around. Unsure of what to say, I headed for the mini-bar. "Would you like something to drink?"

"Yeah, thanks. Mind if I sit down?"

"Oh, how rude of me." I pulled a chair out from under the table. "Please have a seat."

Annie ignored my invitation to the chair and took a seat on the edge of the bed. "Here is fine," she said with a flirtatious smile.

My hands shook as I took two wine coolers out of the minibar and poured them into wine glasses. After handing her one, I quickly stepped back from the bed and stood in front of the window.

"Are you alone?" Annie asked, before taking a sip of her drink.

I took a large swig. "Yes, it's just me."

"You're alone in Vegas? How did that happen?"

I didn't expect Annie to be the one asking the questions, and searched for an answer fast. "My divorce was, um, how do you say it in English? Uh, finalized, and I came to Vegas to celebrate."

"With a woman?"

"Oui. With a woman."

"Are you gay? Is that why you got divorced?"

I shook my head. "No, no, just, er, curious."

Annie moistened her lips with her tongue. "Hmm, so I would be your first woman? Kinky."

I shied away from her sultry stare. "Yes, you are correct. I have never been with a woman before. What about you? Do you like being with a woman?" I finally swallowed the lump in my throat that had been lodged there since her arrival. Asking my husband's sister such a question felt weird.

To my relief, Annie ignored my question and patted the bed. "Look honey, I'm not here to chit-chat. The clock is ticking. Come sit next to me."

I hesitated, as my heart rate elevated and I stared at the floor, then slowly made my way over to the bed. I remained focused on the blue pattern of the rug as I took a seat next to her.

Annie placed her hand on my knee, sending shivers down my spine, and gave it a friendly pat. "Would you like me to kiss you?"

I gasped and pulled my leg away from her hand. "I would like to take it slow, if you don't mind."

Annie shrugged her shoulders and curled her lip. "It's your dime, sweetie."

I gave her a weak smile. "Thank you. I like your dress. Where did you get it?"

Annie released a smirk and looked down at her attire. "Thanks. I got it on sale at some boutique. I fell in love with the colors. Yellow is my favorite."

"I can see why. You are stunningly beautiful. Why do you do this?"

Annie's tone quickly changed to defensive mode. "Look, honey, I'm not here to discuss my personal life. Now, do you want to do this or not?"

"Okay, I'm sorry. Do you mind if I close the bathroom door?"

Annie motioned with her hands for me to go. "Do whatever makes you happy, sweetie."

I quickly stood and marched over to the bathroom, but instead of closing the door, I pushed it open, and Ricky swiftly entered. "So we meet again, Annie," he said, wearing a cocky smile.

Annie's eyes immediately fueled with anger as she hissed her words and raced towards the exit door. "God damn it, Ricky. I told you to leave me the hell alone."

Before she could reach the door, I stood in front of her, blocking her way. "Oh, no you don't. You are not going anywhere."

Annie held out her arms and pushed me hard with the palms of her hands, causing me to fall back against the door. "Get out of my way. You two set me up."

I pushed her back and roared my words at her. "You stole from us and ruined our honeymoon. We want our fucking money back, and Ricky won't leave here without you."

Ricky intervened and grabbed Annie's arm. "Don't you lay a hand on Jill. She has nothing to do with this. This is between you and me."

I disagreed and yelled back. "Yes, I do. The money she took was what I had won, and she took it from my purse."

Ricky turned around and glared at me. "Stay out of this, Jill."

Annie continued to struggle, as Ricky kept a firm grip on her arm. Shaking her body vigorously, she spat out her words at Ricky.

"I am not going anywhere with you. I told you to leave me the hell alone. You will get your money. I have it stashed."

Ricky's grip weakened by the news that she still had the money, and Annie quickly took advantage. She jolted her body, and pulled herself free, while reaching inside her purse, and pulled out a small handgun.

Ricky and I froze, and we immediately raised our hands. Unsure of her next move, my heart pounded.

Annie held the gun tight with both hands as she aimed it at Ricky. "Don't make me use this Ricky," she said, as she inched her way to the door.

Ricky's voice was shaking as he tried to reason with her. "Annie, let's all calm down. I'm your brother." He kept his hands in the air, as he continued to talk to her, "You are not going to shoot me. Come on, put the gun down."

Annie's hands trembled as she continued to walk backwards towards the door, while pointing the gun at Ricky. I was numb and remained frozen with my hands in the air. Ricky matched Annie's steps and remained a few feet away from her, his hands still in the air.

Annie raised her voice. "Don't move Ricky. I swear I will shoot."

Ricky took another step. "No, you won't." He lowered an arm and slowly held out his hand. I held my breath, afraid Annie may shoot him.

Ricky spoke in a gentle voice, focusing on Annie's eyes. "Now, hand me the gun before one of us gets hurt."

Tears pooled in Annie's eyes. Her lips quivered when she spoke through her tears. "Damn it Ricky. Just stay where you are. Please, just let me go."

I lowered my arms and held my hands over my chest. Consumed with fear and uncertainty, my body shook as I thought back to our wedding, when Davin shot Slater.

"Please, put the gun down," I begged, as I leaned against the door. "We are only trying to help."

Annie ignored me and continued to aim the gun at Ricky. I gasped when Ricky took another step toward her.

"Then you will have to shoot me. I can't let you walk out of here," Ricky said, with his hand still held out.

Annie remained silent as she adjusted her hold on the gun and then looked down at her trembling hands. The minute her eyes looked away, Ricky saw an opportunity. He didn't waste a second to react, and with a hard punch aimed at her arm, he knocked the gun out of her hands.

I watched in horror as it fell to the ground, and I immediately raced across the room to kick it away from Annie's reach.

"Watch her!" Ricky yelled, as he grabbed the gun, and quickly unloaded it and threw it on the bed.

Again, Annie pulled herself up and bolted for the door. Rage raced through me, as I lunged at her, and pulled her down to the floor.

"Get off me, bitch," Annie screamed, as I wrestled with her waving arms to keep them from hitting me. Annie arched her back and kicked her legs in the air, barely missing my face, as I fought to keep her at bay. But she was stronger than me, and broke one of her arms free and slapped me hard across the face. My eyes narrowed, as I felt the burning in my cheek, and quickly fired back with a hard slap to her face.

Ricky grabbed my hand and began pulling me off of her. "Okay, that's enough," he yelled, as he yanked me up onto my feet. "Annie, get up and get away from the door," he yelled, with flared nostrils and a piercing stare directed at her.

Annie shook her head and stood. Ricky didn't wait to see what she would do next, and grabbed her arm. Annie tried to pull back as he dragged her over to the table. "Sit down and don't move." He waited until she sat, and then turned to me. "Are you okay?"

I pulled off my wig and shook my hair. "Yeah," I said, as I rubbed my cheek.

He glanced back at Annie, his eyes still wide. "Where the hell did you get a gun? Were you really going to shoot me?"

"One of the girls where I live got it for me. We carry them for protection. There are a lot of weirdos out there."

Ricky shook his head and heaved his chest. "I'm not a weirdo. I'm your brother, and you aimed a gun at me." Ricky wiped the beads of sweat from his brow. "Fuck, Annie."

"I'm sorry, okay. I fucked up and panicked."

"Well, the good thing is no one got hurt, but Jill was right. I'm not leaving without you, Annie. So what's stopping you? Why won't you come with us?"

CHAPTER 21

Annie pulled off her wig and tossed it on the table. "God damn it, Ricky, will you just leave me the hell alone? This is my problem, and I don't want you involved."

Ricky cracked a sarcastic laugh and folded his arms. "Too late. I'm already involved. Now tell me, what is stopping you from just packing your bags and coming home with Jill and me? We are offering you a place to live and helping you escape this hell of a life you have created for yourself."

Annie ran her hands through her hair and released a heavy sigh. "It's not that easy, okay? I'm in the red and I can't just leave. I'm afraid they will come after me for the money I owe, and I don't want to be looking over my shoulder the rest of my life."

Ricky furrowed his brow. "What do you mean, you are in the red? How can you be in the red? I thought they provided everything in lieu of you working for them."

"They do, but everything costs way more than what I make. It's how they keep the girls working for them. They charge double what everything really costs. None of us can break away because we can't save any money. How can we, when they don't pay us in cash, just in food, a roof over our heads, and clothes and stuff?"

With my nerves now settled, I made my way to the table and stood next to Ricky. He took my hand and held it tight as he drilled Annie with more questions. "So that's why you took the five grand out of Jill's purse?"

Annie nodded. "Yes. When I saw it, I couldn't help myself. It was an escape for me. I only wanted the money, which is why I left the purse at the front desk with everything else still in it. I know the headache of losing credit cards, and an ID. It's happened to me many times."

"You said you have the money stashed. Why didn't you give it to the people you work for, and get the hell out of there, if that is what you stole it for?"

Annie lowered her head. "Because it's not enough."

Ricky's jaw dropped. "What? How much do you owe them?"

Annie released a heavy sigh and rubbed her brow. "$7,000. I can't leave without paying it all back."

I could hear the uncertainty in Ricky's tone. "Where is the five grand you said you had stashed? How do I know you are telling us the truth?"

"It's hidden in my car, buried in the back seat. It's the only place I know for sure that no one will search. I have no idea if they go through my room when I am not there."

Ricky let go of my hand and began pacing the room. "So, if you pay them what you owe, will you be able to walk away from that place?"

"Yes, I would," Annie replied.

"And they would let you go?" I added.

Annie nodded. "Yes. I've seen other girls pay up and leave."

"Okay then. Then that's what we are going to do. We will give you the other $2,000, and you are going to take us to wherever it is you live, and pay them. "

Annie shook her head. "No Ricky, I can't let you do that. I already owe you enough."

"Yeah, but I'm not telling you to sleep with men to pay me back. Like the jerks you work for. Now get up. We are going to take your car, and you are going to show me the money before we leave."

Annie's eyes grew wide. "Ricky, you can't go to the house. No men are allowed there."

"I don't give a shit about their rules and I'm not letting you out of my sight. I'm not sure if I can trust you," he said, as he walked over to the bed and picked up the gun. He glanced around the room and grabbed our luggage. I watched as he stuffed the gun underneath our clothes before zipping the bag closed. "Now come on, get up. We are out of here." He looked my way. "We will be back later to get the rest of our stuff. We are leaving Vegas tonight," he said in a stern voice.

CHAPTER 22

Ricky didn't let go of Annie's arm as we made our way to the parking lot of the hotel. I walked close behind him, unsure of his plans. I was confused by what he meant. We were leaving tonight. We hadn't had a chance to be alone and discuss what his plans were. I was simply going along with everything, but I wondered, what happens when we are home? Ricky told Annie she could stay with us, but I'm not comfortable with the idea at all. What about my feelings? I barely know her, and I sure as hell don't trust her. Ricky and I needed to talk.

Annie led us to a dark blue Toyota. "Hand me your keys," Ricky insisted. "I'll drive."

Annie unlocked the car and handed him the keys. "Do you want me in the front or back?" she asked.

"In the front." Ricky snapped. "But before we get in, show me the money. You said it was stashed in your car."

Ricky and I waited outside the car while Annie opened the backdoor, squeezed her hand down between the seat and backrest, and pulled out a manila envelope. "Here. It's all there," Annie said, as she handed the envelope to Ricky.

Ricky gave me the envelope. "Count this Jill, while we are driving."

Annie rolled her eyes. "What, you don't trust me?"

I cracked a loud laugh. "Give me one reason why we should?" I asked with sarcasm before getting in the car, where I immediately started counting the cash.

Before putting our bag in the trunk, Ricky opened it and pulled out the unloaded gun. "Annie, put this in your purse."

Annie creased her brow. "Why?"

"Because I don't want it anywhere near me. You are going to leave it somewhere in your room, or give it back to the girl who gave it to you. It's not registered in your name, is it?"

"No."

"Good, then you are going to get rid of it. But you do know that it's illegal to carry an unlicensed gun, don't you? "

Annie shrugged her shoulders. "It's a risk I'm willing to take to protect myself."

Ricky put the car in gear and headed toward the exit. "We need to go to an ATM and get out more cash. Jill, you can take out $1,000 out of your bank and I'll take $1,000 out of mine."

I gasped. "What? I'm already out $5,000," I hollered from the back seat.

Ricky glared at me through the rearview mirror. "I have a $1,000 daily limit on my ATM withdrawal. I'll pay you back."

"How? And who is going to pay me back the $5,000? This really sucks, you know. We have rent coming up soon, and I'm not getting any more money from my parents, remember? I didn't plan on starting my marriage in debt, Ricky."

Annie turned her head, giving me a hard stare. "I said I would pay you back."

I narrowed my eyes at her and spat out my words. "Shut up, okay. It's because of you that we are in this mess. Your words mean nothing to me."

Ricky raised his voice to match my tone. "Okay, that's enough.

I'll get a front from Slater when we get home. I'll work it out, okay?"

After counting the money, I put it back in the envelope. "The money is all there."

"I told you," Annie snapped.

"Will you just shut up!" I hollered.

"Jill, I said, that's enough." Ricky shouted back. He then spoke to Annie. "Annie, tell me where there is an ATM."

When we pulled up to the bank, we made our withdrawals separately, so one of us could stay in the car with Annie. Ricky handed me his cash and, together with mine, I added it to the money in the envelope.

After leaving the bank, I remained quiet in the back seat, while Annie gave Ricky directions to where she lived. I looked out the window at the darkened streets that were now much quieter than those in the heart of Vegas.

We had been driving for about twenty minutes, and were now in a residential area with rows of townhouses. Annie told Ricky to turn right and pointed to the third house on the right. "That's it," she said, while pointing out the window.

Ricky scanned the street. "Not a bad neighborhood."

"We have to blend in Ricky, and trust me, the girls and I pay for it. How do you think I got $7,000 in the red?"

Ricky turned off the car in front of the house next door. "Okay, let's do this," he said in a stern voice, while yanking the keys out of the ignition.

"I told you, no men are allowed in there, Ricky."

"And I told you, I don't give a shit. I'm not letting you out of my sight. Now come on, get out." He turned his head and looked at me. "Come on, Jill. I'm not leaving you out here alone."

Ricky got out of the car first, and opened my door, before going around to the passenger side, where he waited for Annie to get out.

"Hand me the envelope, Jill," Ricky said, as we walked up the driveway.

Ricky stayed close to Annie as we approached the front door. "Do you have a key?" Ricky asked.

"Yes."

"Open the door," Ricky ordered, as I stood nervously behind him.

Annie did as she was told and unlocked the door. As soon as she pushed it open, Ricky barged in and hollered. "Who's in charge here?"

Before I entered the house, I heard a few screams and saw three girls sitting on the couch in pajamas watching a movie. Two quickly stood up and faced us. The other remained seated, and someone called out a name, "Savanna!."

"No men allowed here. What do you want?" one girl yelled.

Annie raised her hand. "It's okay, he's with me. He's my brother."

A middle-aged woman appeared from another room. She gave Ricky a hard stare. "What the hell are you doing here?" She turned and looked at Annie. "Carina, you know the rules. No men allowed."

Ricky took Annie's hand and marched over to the woman. "Who are you? And I'm not just any man. I'm her brother, and her name is Annie, and she is leaving here tonight."

"I'm Savanna, and I'm in charge here." She looked over at Annie. "Is this true? You want to leave?"

Ricky raised his voice and spoke before Annie had a chance. "Yes, she does." He held up the envelope. "There's enough money in here to pay off what she owes you. Though she shouldn't owe you a dime. She's been working for you for quite a while. You, and whoever your boss is, are taking advantage of these women. Now, I don't want any problems. She needs to get her things and then we will be gone."

"Well, I have to check the books."

Ricky spat out his next words. "Look, lady. Annie told me what she owes you, and that is what we have in here. Count it right now, while Annie grabs her things." He let go of Annie's hand. "Go on, Annie." He looked over at me. "Jill, you go with her, and I'll stay here while this lady counts the money."

I quickly ushered Annie away and followed her up the stairs. She led me to a small room at the end of the hallway and opened the door. It was a simple room with a bed, nightstand, and a dresser with a large mirror. There were posters of Vegas on the wall, and makeup and creams adorned the dresser, along with a few wigs.

"Hurry up and get your stuff," I told her.

Annie pulled a bag from the closet and began filling it up with clothes and a few items on the dresser. "You don't like me, do you?" she said, while stuffing clothes in her bag.

I stood by the door with my arms folded. "Can you blame me?"

"Look, I did what I had to do to survive, okay?" Annie snapped.

"Yeah, at my expense, I might add."

Annie threw a handful of underwear into the bag. "Will you get off your high horse for just one minute? I bet you probably got everything handed to you on a silver platter, and never had to struggle a day in your life. If you had to live my life, you'd be dead." She threw more items into the bag and then turned to look at me. "Did Ricky ever tell you about our lives growing up?"

I shook my head, "No."

"We had it rough, okay? When our dad left with one of his bimbos, it was just us and our mom. She raised me and Ricky while working two jobs. She could barely put food on the table. We lived off noodles and spaghetti sauce out of a can. Ricky was a shy, withdrawn kid with low self-esteem. It wasn't until he started working for your friend Slater when he was in his teens that he turned his life around and felt confident about himself."

"Look, I'm sorry. I had no idea. Ricky never told me. I met your mom. She seems so happy."

"Well, yeah, Tony, her boyfriend, came into the picture, and things got much better for her, but not for me. Every day I lived in fear with my asshole boyfriend Adam, until I couldn't take it anymore, and left, and ended up here."

"Why didn't you leave him sooner?" I asked.

Annie rolled her eyes and shook her head. "If it was that easy I would have, but I was afraid to." She flung her bag over her shoulder. "I bet you have no friggin idea what living in fear is like."

She left the wigs and a lot of the makeup behind. After grabbing her purse, she released a heavy sigh. "Let's get out of here."

I scanned the room. "You're leaving the rest behind?"

"Yep. I have no use for it. The other girls will come in here and grab what they want."

"Where's the girl that gave you the gun?" I asked.

"She's working."

"Well, then leave it somewhere, like Ricky asked. I'm sure she will find it, or someone will."

I watched as Annie pulled the gun out of her purse and placed it on the top shelf of the closet.

Satisfied, I opened the door. "Okay, let's go."

CHAPTER 23

When we returned downstairs, the girls were back to watching the TV. A petite blonde turned her head and looked over the back of the couch. Ricky was nowhere to be found. "So, you are really leaving, eh?" the blonde said, while looking at Annie.

Annie nodded and walked over to the girls. "Yeah. Little brother's orders."

I watched as the four girls stood in a group hug, and was touched by the friendship they shared. It was genuine. Even though we didn't approve of Annie's lifestyle, I sensed these women were like family to her. They all had each other's back. One had even given her a gun. I felt pity for the other girls that Annie was leaving behind, but maybe they chose to do what they did and were not forced to, in order to survive, like Annie. I was unsure if Annie and I could ever be that close after what she had done to us.

"Has anyone seen Ricky?" I asked from across the room.

The blonde broke away from Annie and the rest of the girls,

pointing to a door behind me. "They are in the office. I'm sure they will be out in a few minutes."

I stood nervously by the front door, while Annie continued to say her goodbyes. Just like the girl had said, the door opened, and Ricky appeared. I rushed to him and took his hand. "Can we go now?"

Ricky squeezed my hand. "Yeah, we are all done here." He looked over my shoulder. "Come on Annie, let's go."

Annie looked up, giving the girls one last hug.

The head of the house intervened, and spoke to Annie, " before you leave, can I talk to you in my office?"

Ricky quickly marched over to Annie and grabbed her hands. "Oh, no you don't. Whatever you have to say, you can say it right here."

Annie pulled away from Ricky's hold, and walked over to the older woman, who placed her hands on Annie's shoulders. "You will always have a place here. Take care of yourself, okay?"

Annie nodded and handed the woman a cell phone. I assumed it was her work phone. "I will."

Ricky released a sarcastic laugh. "Yeah, I'm sure you will welcome her back with open arms, with all the money you are making off these women." He walked over to Annie and took her hand. "Come on, let's go."

When we reached Annie's car, we all sat in the same seats. Annie leaned back in the front seat and folded her arms. "Happy now?" she said in a sharp tone.

Ricky turned to face Annie. "No, I'm not happy. We are out $7,000, and suddenly, I have to play babysitter for my big sister."

Annie leaned forward and scowled at Ricky. "Hey, I never asked for your help. I was doing just fine on my own."

"You call this doing fine, Annie? And if you were doing so well, why the hell did you steal from Jill?"

"I told you, I would pay you back. Just give me some time to get my shit together, okay?"

I remained quiet in the back seat, while Ricky started up the car and pulled away from the curb. I knew little about Annie and Ricky's childhood, except for what Annie had told me, and wondered if they were close growing up? Had Annie been protective of Ricky because she was the eldest? It seemed if that were the case, it had now been reversed. Ricky had come to his sister's rescue. Their relationship was now suffering from all the events that had happened this week. I wondered if it could ever be saved? Or, more importantly, could we ever trust Annie again?

We were all lost in our own private thoughts, and didn't share many words on the drive back to the Bellagio. When we pulled into the parking garage, Ricky spoke. "We are going to grab our things, and Jill, I want you to call the car rental place at the airport and tell them we are dropping off our rental tonight."

I creased my brow. "Why?"

"Because we are leaving tonight and driving back to San Diego in Annie's car. We can't leave it here."

"We are going to drive all the way back to San Diego?" I protested.

"Yes. What choice do we have?" Ricky explained. "Annie will need her car to look for a job."

I flopped back in my seat and moaned. "God, this honeymoon keeps getting worse. How long will it take us to drive?"

"About five hours, and we will have to stop for breaks and food." Ricky replied.

"And I guess when we get home, Annie will be staying with us?"

"Well, yes. We had already discussed this, Jill. Annie has nowhere to go."

"We didn't talk about it, Ricky. You told me. You didn't even ask me how I felt about all of this."

Ricky gave Annie a quick glance, who sat in silence next to him with her arms folded. "Can we talk about this later? Why are you suddenly making this difficult when we have gone to all this trouble getting Annie out of that place?"

"When are we supposed to talk about it, Ricky? We no longer have any privacy to discuss anything."

Annie intervened. "Do you want me to leave?"

Ricky grabbed her arm. "You are not going anywhere." He turned and looked at me. "Jill, it will just be for a little while. We'll talk more about it on the drive home. All three of us need to be on the same page. We all need to get along."

$\mathcal{I}$t didn't take us long to gather our things from the room at the Bellagio and check out. Twenty minutes later, we were on our way to Caesars Palace to get the rest of our things, checkout, and return the car rental.

"You can drive the rental to the airport, and I will follow you in Annie's car," Ricky said, after handing me the keys in the parking lot.

I took the keys and moaned. "I'm so tired. What time is it?" I released a heavy sigh. "I can't believe we have to drive to San Diego tonight."

"It's almost one in the morning. You can sleep for a few hours while I drive, and then you can drive, so I can take a nap," Ricky told me.

"And I guess Annie gets to sleep the whole way," I said, before walking towards the rental.

Ricky shook his head and didn't bother to reply, then got in the driver's seat of Annie's car, where she was waiting.

After dropping off the rental, I opened the back door of Annie's car. "You can sit up front if you want and Annie can sit in the back," Ricky said before I got in.

"No," I said in a sharp tone, feeling exhausted. "I want to stretch out on the back seat. Wake me up when it's my turn to drive."

I must have fallen asleep straight away, because the next thing I remember was Ricky leaning in the back door, kissing me on my lips. "Hey sleeping beauty, wake up," I heard him whisper.

I tried to stretch, but the confined space of the back seat wouldn't allow me. I then remembered where I was and why I was in the car. My mood suddenly turned sour. I was still living this nightmare. The car was stopped, and a bright street lamp illuminated the inside of the car. I rubbed my eyes and sat up. "Where are we?" I asked, while looking out the window.

"A gas station. Do you feel like driving?" Ricky replied.

I looked over at the front seat and saw Annie was sleeping. "Why can't she drive? It's her car."

"I'd rather she didn't. She may take a detour or something." He shrugged his shoulders. "I dunno. Let me just say, I'm still unsure of her," he whispered, before standing away from the door so I could get out.

We stood outside of the car, and I wrapped my arms around my waist, shivering from the sudden chill of the cool morning air. "I need some coffee."

"Okay, I'll run inside and get you one. Are you hungry?"

I shook my head. "No."

By the time Ricky returned, I was sitting in the driver's seat. He handed me the coffee, and the aroma of the freshly brewed drink stimulated my sinuses, as well as my sleepy state. I took a sip and smacked my lips. "Thanks. That tastes good."

Ricky got in the back seat. "Wake me up in an hour."

While driving in silence with the other two passengers asleep, I wondered how all of this was going to work out. I had so much resentment towards Annie that I wasn't sure if I'd ever be able to let them go. The idea of her living with us and supporting her until she got her life together was not sitting well with me. How long would we have to babysit her, feed her, and cater to all her needs? All for free. How much more do I have to give of myself? I'm trying to get rid of the old Jill and be a nice person, considerate of others, but this is asking too much. The old Jill would have handled this much better. I laughed out loud at my thoughts, and told myself, the old Jill would never have put up with this shit. Hell, she would never have let it get this far. It suddenly occurred to me, if I hadn't changed my ways, Ricky and I may have split up. Knowing my old self, I knew without a doubt, my self-centered ways and temper would have definitely severed our relationship.

My phone rang, pulling me away from my thoughts. I gave the screen a quick glance and saw it was my mom calling. She lived in Spain, so I assumed it was early afternoon for her. I spun the phone face down and tried to erase the thoughts of my mom out of my head, but failed. This was the third call from her since we arrived in Vegas. She had left a voicemail after each one, but I'd refused to listen to them. Not only because we were dealing with Annie, but because I'm not ready to. I'm not even sure if I ever will be. If I decide to talk to her, I have to be just as strong as I was when I finally stood up to her in the lounge the day before our wedding. She didn't know how to handle it and left, without saying a word, and never came to our wedding. I was also disappointed with my dad, who never stood up for me and has never called me to see how I was doing.

I won't be caught in her web again. I have finally found myself, and she needs to let me be, accept me for who I am and not try to spin me into a younger version of herself. I cringed at the thought that I had been on that path until Travis's accident caused me to look at myself differently.

The phone rang again. I flipped it over and saw it was my mom again. She was getting persistent now. I wasn't being the way I had always acted in the past. Which was to call her back right away, and say only what I knew she wanted to hear. Not anymore mom, those days are over. You hurt me, and I'm not sure if I ever want to speak to you again.

CHAPTER 25

The ringing of my phone stirred Annie from her sleep. She wiped her eyes and pulled herself up from her slouched position, glancing out at the darkness. "Where are we?"

"About two hours from home," I said, not taking my eyes off the road.

"Do you want me to drive?"

"No, Ricky doesn't want you to. Like me, he doesn't trust you."

"You know, if I'm going to be living with you guys, you better start putting some trust in me."

I narrowed my eyes and gave her a quick, hard stare. "You don't make it that easy."

Annie released a heavy sigh. "Look Jill, I know we got off to a wrong start."

"I'll say," I interrupted.

"Will you let me finish?" She paused, anticipating I had more to say, but I remained quiet and she continued to speak. "Will you give me another chance? I may not show it, but I appreciate what you and Ricky have done. I saw the money I took from you as my way out of the hellhole I've been living. That's how desperate I was to break away from the life I had gotten myself trapped into. It's how they keep the girls working for them. We are continually in the red and make no real cash. So when I saw all that money, I couldn't help myself. I promise you, I will pay you back every cent. I'm not a bad person. Just someone who's been dealt a lot of shit in her life. I appreciate everything you guys have done."

Her words took me by surprise. They sounded genuine, and I wasn't sure how to react. I gave her a weak smile. "I just need some time, okay?"

She matched my smile. "That's all I'm asking for."

About an hour from our place, we stopped for breakfast, and it was there that Annie asked Ricky a question that hadn't crossed my mind. "Are you going to tell mom?"

"No, I think I'll leave that up to you. Do you plan on telling her?" Ricky replied.

"I don't know Ricky. It would break her heart if she found out her daughter worked for an escort service in Las Vegas. It's why I kept all of this from you."

"Then don't tell her."

"Well, how are we going to explain to her, us running into each other, and that I'm now living with you? I don't want to start another stream of lies and drag you into covering for me."

Ricky gave his sister a caring smile that touched my heart and took her hand. "Look Annie, we don't have to tell her right away. It's not like we see mom every day. Get settled in first at our place. When you are ready to talk to her, we will go over together what you want to tell her and how much."

"Thanks. I love you. You are the best brother."

"And I love you. Even though you pulled a gun on me," he chuckled.

"I would never have shot you, Ricky."

Ricky grinned. "I know that." He picked up the check. "Come on, ladies, let's get out of here. We are almost home."

We arrived home exhausted and dragged our tired bodies

inside. I never felt more pleased to be home, but enjoying the simple comforts would have to wait a few more hours. I needed to lay my head on my pillow and feel my pink satin sheets embrace my body. When I wake up in the morning, I would call Sadie and arrange to pick up Maggie.

After showing Annie the guest room, Ricky followed me into our room, and within minutes, we were naked under the covers, asleep in each other's arms.

I'm not sure how long I had been asleep, but I woke up to the sound of a high-pitched scream, and the smell of smoke. At first I thought I was dreaming, and repositioned my body in a more comfy state, but then I heard the chilling screams again. My eyes instantly opened, and I bolted out of bed. "Ricky, wake up! I smell smoke," I screamed, as I raced to the door, grabbed my robe, and charged out of the room. Ricky was soon behind me, still tying the belt of his robe around his waist.

I didn't knock on the door of the guest room, and instead, pushed the door open with force. "My god, what the hell happened?" I screamed, covering my mouth with my hand from the choking smoke that engulfed the room. Annie screamed again as she beat the burning pillow with another pillow.

She stared at us with fear in her eyes. "My pillow is on fire. I can't put it out," she screamed in a panicked state. "Help me!"

Ricky pushed me aside and raced to the bed. "Don't beat it. You are just fueling the fire," he yelled, while scanning the room with wide eyes. "We need water." He raced into the guest bathroom and threw the contents of the trash can on the floor before bolting over to the bathtub and filling it with water.

I ran from the bedroom and into our bathroom, and did the same with our trash can. Annie grabbed a large empty vase off the dresser and joined Ricky in the bathroom.

"Fill it up fast," he yelled, as he passed her with a full trash can of water, and threw the contents onto the pillow.

My heart raced as I entered the room. The smoke from the

dampened fire filled the air, and I coughed hard to clear my lungs. Ricky quickly grabbed my trash can and threw the water on the smoldering pillow. More smoke filled the room, and we both coughed and tried to cover our mouths. Annie entered the room and handed Ricky the vase, which he immediately emptied onto the pillow.

"Get more water!" he yelled, as he threw a trash can at Annie, and smothered the pillow with the quilt. I grabbed the second trash can and returned to our bathroom. By the time I had returned, Annie had already given Ricky another trash can full of water, which he had poured onto the bed. He quickly grabbed the one I was carrying and drenched the blanket on top of the pillow. Smoke choked the room, and I covered my nose and mouth, then stood outside in the hallway where I could breathe.

Ricky's chest heaved as he pressed down hard on the soaked blanket covering the smoldering pillow. "I think it's out," he yelled.

Annie joined me in the hallway, and I gave her a fierce stare. "What the hell happened?" I screamed.

Tears ran down her cheeks as she coughed and struggled to talk. "I don't know. I must have fallen asleep with a cigarette. I'm so sorry. It was an accident."

I could feel my blood boiling as I raised my voice to a harsh scream. "You were smoking! We specifically asked you not to smoke in the house. You could have burnt down our home or even worse, killed us."

I cannot remember ever feeling such anger towards someone. "What the hell were you thinking?" I yelled, and then the doorbell rang. "Great! Now we have woken up the neighbors."

I stormed down the stairs and paused before opening the door. I needed to calm my nerves, and the anger I was feeling, so I took a few deep breaths before facing whoever was on the other side of the door. After my heart rate had returned to somewhat normal, I opened the door, and there was my neighbor to greet me, Hazel, who was dressed in a blue bathrobe and lived in the condo next door.

"Jill, is everything okay? I thought I heard a scream coming from here."

I nodded. "Yeah, everything is fine. Ricky's sister is staying with us, and she had a nightmare. Sorry it woke you."

Hazel looked over my shoulder as she spoke. "Okay, then. I just wanted to make sure you were okay. I thought you weren't coming back from Vegas for a few more days?"

"A change of plans. We will talk soon. Goodnight Hazel," I said, as I inched the door towards her.

"Okay. Goodnight."

I leaned my back against the closed door and closed my eyes. My anger was returning. I couldn't do this anymore, and stormed back upstairs. I found Annie and Ricky sitting on the edge of the dry side of the bed. Smoke still lingered in the room. I remained in the doorway, my body trembling as I spoke. "Annie, I want you out of here. In the morning, I want you to pack your things and get out."

Ricky's jaw dropped. "Now wait a minute Jill, it was an accident."

I raised my voice. "I want her out of here tomorrow." Without waiting for a reply, I stormed off to our room, slamming the door.

CHAPTER 26

*R*icky entered the room about ten minutes later. I was already under the covers, with the sheets pulled up over my shoulders. I didn't acknowledge his presence, and laid with my back towards him. Awake, but with my eyes closed, I listened as he undressed and crawled into bed next to me, and wrapped his arm around my waist. His hands were cold against my bare skin.

"Are you awake?" he whispered.

"Yes," I answered in a flat tone.

"You didn't mean what you said, did you?"

I rolled over on my back, resting my forearm across my brow. "Yes, I did. I don't want her here, Ricky."

"But she has nowhere to go, Jill."

"And we won't have a house if she stays. She doesn't respect anything we ask of her, and I just don't trust her or feel safe with her staying here."

Ricky rubbed my shoulder. "Don't you think you are being a bit irrational? It was an honest mistake. She fell asleep."

I sat up and folded my arms, while giving Ricky a hard stare. "I can't believe you are defending her. We made it clear to her when we pulled into our driveway that we didn't want her to smoke in our home. She completely ignored us and almost burnt down our house. It wasn't a mistake, Ricky. She went against our wishes."

Ricky pulled his hand away and released a heavy sigh. "Well, where do you expect her to go?"

"That is not our problem. We are not her caregivers. I have been making sacrifices all week for that woman, and I'm not about to put my home and peace of mind on the line because she has no respect for anyone but herself, why the hell should I?"

"So you don't want to help her?"

My anger was rising again, and I stormed out of the bed. "I have been helping her all week. What more do you want from me? This entire week has been a nightmare. We were supposed to be on our honeymoon. What a great way to start a marriage." I marched over to the door, grabbed my bathrobe, and gave him a harsh stare as I pulled it on with force. "I'm going to pick up Maggie in the morning. When I get back, I want her gone."

"Where are you going?" Ricky asked, as I opened the door.

"To sleep on the couch," I yelled, before slamming the door shut.

After grabbing some blankets from the closet, I made myself comfy on the couch, and texted Sadie to see if I could pick up Maggie early in the morning before she left for work. I didn't want to be here when Annie or Ricky woke up, and set the alarm for six.

I must have fallen asleep straight away, because the sound of my alarm going off was the next thing I remember. I quickly shut it off before it would wake Annie or Ricky and then checked my messages. There was nothing from Sadie. I assumed she wasn't up yet and hadn't seen the message. Not wanting to sit around and risk still being home when Ricky and Annie woke up, I pulled some clean clothes out of our luggage bags that we still hadn't unpacked. After washing my face, I made do with the makeup I had in my purse. After brushing my hair, I chugged down a glass of orange juice, grabbed my phone and purse, and headed out the door.

Two blocks away from home, my phone pinged. It was a message from Sadie. I quickly pulled over to check her message. She asked if everything was okay, and confirmed I could pick up Maggie. I called her back rather than texting.

After a few rings, she answered. "Hey Jill, is everything okay? You're back early."

"Yeah, I'm fine. Just a change of plans. I'm on my way."

"Wow, you are up early. I don't have to be at work until noon. You can come later if you want. There's no rush."

"No, I want to see Maggie. I've missed her. Besides, I don't want to be at home right now."

"What's going on Jill? Is everything okay between you and Ricky?"

I released a heavy sigh. "I'll fill you in when I get there. Put some coffee on."

By the time I reached Sadie's, my phone had rung twice. It was Ricky, and I ignored his calls. Instead, I texted him when I pulled into Sadie's and Logan's driveway.

I'm picking up Maggie and visiting with Sadie. Text me when Annie is gone and I will come home.

He replied with one word—*Fine.*

As soon as Sadie opened her front door, Maggie pushed her way through and raced outside, greeting me with joyful barks and a rambunctious wagging tail. "Maggie!" I yelled, as I knelt and took her in my arms, I beamed a huge smile as she covered my face in mounds of licks and pushed her head into my lap. "I've missed you, girl."

Maggie kept close to my side as I walked into Sadie's home and gave her a hug. "Thank you so much for taking care of her." I scanned the front room and across to the open kitchen. "Where's Logan?"

"He left early. There's some event going on at the beach, so he is opening his store early."

"How's the surfboard business going?" I asked, as we walked toward the kitchen.

"It's doing really well. Then again, we are at the peak of summer. September may slow down a bit." She pointed to the table. "Have a seat. I'll bring you a cup of coffee, and you can tell me what's going on."

Maggie followed me over to the table and made herself comfy at my feet. I continued to pet her while Sadie filled two mugs with coffee and joined me at the table.

"So why are you back early? What's going on?" Sadie asked, before taking a swig of her coffee.

I cracked a sarcastic laugh. "How much time do you have? It's been an awful week." I gave Sadie the rundown of my honeymoon in Vegas up to the fire last night.

The entire time, Sadie listened with a dropped jaw, announcing her disbelief before allowing me to continue. "My god. I'm so sorry. It sounds like she pretty much ruined your honeymoon. Well, I'm glad she didn't come to the wedding. She would have ruined that, too, I'm sure," Sadie said, with a quick shake of her head. "Even though that guy, Davin, managed to do that. Hey, speaking of which, have you heard anything from Slater? Is he doing okay?" Sadie asked.

"Yeah. he's home now and taking it easy."

"Do you think Ricky's sister will move out today?" Sadie asked, while refilling our coffee.

"She doesn't have a choice. I don't want her there, and I told Ricky to text me when she's gone. I'm not going home until she has left. She brings the worst out in me, I swear."

"So I guess you'll never see that seven grand again?"

"I don't care. I just want her out of my life."

"Yeah, but that's a lot of money, Jill."

"Yeah, well, you can't get water out of a stone. I'm sure she had no plans to pay us back. Look at all the other shit she did to us."

Sadie nodded. "Yeah, I guess you are right. Well, you and Maggie are free to stay here until the coast is clear. You can just lock up if I have to leave for work. All of Maggie's stuff is packed, and by the front door."

"Thanks, I appreciate it."

"So how is married life with you and Logan? I still can't believe you eloped," I laughed.

Her eyes didn't hide the happiness she felt, and her smile confirmed it. "It's amazing. I don't regret a thing. Logan is wonderful, and he treats me like a queen. Something I'm still trying to get used to. We are definitely getting a dog, by the way. We have Maggie to thank for that. It's been great having her here, and we are going to check out some shelters this weekend."

"It's good to see you happy. You guys make a great couple."

Sadie reached out and took my hand. "And so do you and Ricky. Once his sister is out of the picture, you guys will be just fine. It's good you were honest with Ricky."

"Do you think so? You don't think I'm being a little too hard?"

"No, not all. Why should you be unhappy in your own home? Ricky needs to think about your needs, too. Not just Annie's. I understand she is his sister, but you are his wife. Who knows how long she would stay there if you didn't put your foot down? It may have dragged on for months, if not years. It may have even split you and Ricky up. No, what you did was the right thing."

"Thanks, I needed to hear that."

"What about your mom? Have you spoken to her since your fallout?"

I shook my head. "No. She's texted me a few times, but I don't know what to say to her. She really hurt me, and it was the day before my wedding. How could she be so cold?"

"I don't know your mom. I've never met her. But I've heard the stories you have told me about her, and you always ended them the same way."

I creased my brow. "I did? How?"

"You always said, I can't pick my parents. That's who they are. It's just their weird way of showing me they care about me."

I shrugged my shoulders. "Yeah, I guess I said that a lot. I was always covering for them."

Sadie shook her head. "No, you accepted them for who they are. Your mother loves you. We both know that. She just hasn't figured out the right way to show it. Maybe this little fall out you had will bring that out in her."

"Oh, I don't know. You don't know my mom. This will be all my fault, and I can assure you that she will demand an apology before we try to fix anything."

"So you are not against making amends with your mom?"

"I didn't say that."

"Yes, you did. You said, before you try to fix anything. That tells me you want to."

I leaned back in my chair, and Maggie instantly sat up, anticipating me leaving again. I immediately began petting her, to reassure her I was not. "Oh, I don't know. We fought in the past, but nothing like this. It's the first time I've actually stood up to her and let her know what I think."

"And that's a good thing. She probably needed to hear it. I'm sure she's never seen herself the way you do. Look how you've changed. It took Travis's accident to see yourself in your true colors. Well, maybe this is what your mom needed. Let her think about what you said for a while, and then make that call. But I think not rushing is a good thing. It gives both of you time to think and miss each other."

I laughed. "Miss her? I can assure you., I do not miss her nagging ways."

"Oh, yes, you do. You just don't know it yet. But you will, and that is when you will make that call."

Sadie stood from the table. "Hey, let's take Maggie for a walk. I normally do before I go to work."

"Sounds good, and thanks so much for listening to my woes."

Sadie gave me a caring smile. "That's what friends are for."

CHAPTER 27

After returning from our walk, Sadie grabbed a large cup of coffee to go. "Make yourself at home. I'm meeting Logan after work, so we won't be home until after dark."

"Say hi to everyone at work. I'll be back next week."

"Good, we've missed you. Text me when you hear anything from Ricky." She knelt down and gave Maggie a hug, and allowed her to lick her face. "I'm going to miss you, girl."

After Sadie had left, I made another cup of coffee, and snuggled with Maggie on the couch, but not before removing the cow hide from behind me. The thought of leaning against it made me cringe, and my skin itch. I glanced around the room. I had only been here once before, when Logan and Sadie had first met. When she moved out of my place, I helped bring over some of her things. Not much had changed. Logan's prized surfboards still hung on the wall above the TV, and pictures of men surfing giant waves hung on the other two walls. Sadie had added her western touch with a few animal hides, a rustic wooden coffee table, and a horse-shoe coat rack by the front door.

I sat idle with my legs crossed and my arms folded, wondering what I was going to do with myself. I thought about going to the gym to release some of the aggression I felt, but soon realized I had no workout clothes with me.

Within minutes, Maggie was asleep with her head in my lap. I leaned down and kissed the top of her head. "We'll go home soon, girl. I just need that bitch to be gone." I checked the time and saw it was almost 10 and decided to call Sabela to check in.

"Hey Jill. How is the honeymoon going?" she asked, in a chirpy voice.

"Oh, don't ask. We came back last night. It was a nightmare. We ran into Ricky's sister in Vegas, and she ruined the whole thing. I can't stand her."

I heard one of the twins crying in the background. "Hold on a second, let me grab Joy. It's her feeding time. I've gotten pretty good at multitasking," she laughed.

A few minutes later, Sabela returned to the line. "Sorry about that. She's happy now. I have her propped up on one arm. So tell me what's going on? Did she tell you why she couldn't make it to the wedding? Is that why you hate her?"

"Oh, it's a bunch of stuff. I'm at Sadie's right now because she almost burned our house down when she fell asleep with a cigarette. And that was after we had asked her not to smoke in the house. Can you believe that?"

I could hear the confusion in Sabela's voice. "Wait, she's staying with you?"

"Not for long. I told Ricky I'm not coming home until she is gone. Ricky is trying to save her. She was working for an escort service in Las Vegas, oh, and she stole $5,000 from us. I have never been so pissed."

"Shit! You're kidding. I'm sorry Jill. What a way to spend your honeymoon and start your marriage. You and Ricky are okay, I hope? Don't let her come between you. You guys make a great couple."

"She already has. It's been all about Annie all week. I mean it, Sabela. I'm not going home until she is gone."

"How long did Sadie say you could stay?"

I hesitated. "Well, she didn't exactly. I'm hoping Annie is gone today sometime."

"Well, where is she going to go, Jill? She has no friends in San Diego, and I'm guessing she left her boyfriend in LA, so she can't go there."

"You sound like Ricky." I raised my voice a notch. "I have no idea where she is going to go, and I honestly don't care. I just want my life back when it was just me and Ricky. Why are you defending her?"

"I'm not. Just logic, that's all. From what you are telling me, she has nowhere to go, Jill."

I felt frustrated by Sabela's lack of sympathy for the way I was feeling, but realized she was right, which I refused to acknowledge. "Can we please change the subject? How are the kids? How is Slater doing?"

I sensed her smile when she spoke. "Slater is doing great. The wound is healing really well, he is slowly easing back into work. He's been helping with the girls a lot, along with my mom, who is here every day," she laughed. "She can't stay away. Scottie is in school and Hope is sleeping. Joy should go down soon. They are growing so fast. After you get your life sorted, you and Ricky should come for dinner."

"We would love that."

I heard crying in the background again, and Sabela cut our conversation short. "Hey, I gotta go. Joy is fussing. Call me soon, okay?"

"Sure," I replied, feeling disappointed she had to go. After I ended the call, I released a heavy sigh, then leaned back and closed my eyes. As I drifted off to sleep, I thought about what Sadie had said about my mom, and questioned if she was right. Was I missing my mom? We didn't have the best mother-daughter relationship, but it was all we had. Maybe there was some truth to what Sadie had said. Maybe my mom's nagging and condescending ways were the only way to show me she cared. I fought with the idea of calling her, and possibly making amends, but decided against it. Our last encounter scared me, and the fact that she would rather miss my wedding than try to fix our fallout. I had no idea what I would say to her in the back of my head. I kept telling myself that she needed to make the first move, but I feared she had too much pride, and never would.

Maggie woke me about an hour later with a sharp, frustrated bark. As soon as I sat up and rubbed my eyes, she jumped off the couch and ran to the back door, letting me know she had to go outside. I left the door open so she could come and go as she pleased, and spent the next few hours moping around Sadie's place, feeling sorry for myself. I tried watching some TV, read a few Country Home magazines off the coffee table, which didn't appeal to me, and played with Maggie.

While playing ball with Maggie in the backyard, my phone rang, and I raced to the patio table and saw it was Ricky. I answered the call in the hopes he had some good news.

"Well?" I said in a sharp tone. "Is she gone?"

I heard a heavy sigh. "She will be gone in the morning. She is going to our mother's."

"Then I will come back tomorrow," I proclaimed.

"Jill, just come home. She will be out of here tomorrow. It's the earliest flight I could get. She's really sorry."

"I don't care how sorry she is. I'm not coming home until she is gone. So, what did you tell your mom?"

"Everything," Ricky replied in a flat tone. "We didn't hide anything. Annie is tired of lying, and didn't want to stay with mom unless she knew the truth."

"How did your mom take it?"

"She was upset, of course, but was eager to help Annie get back on her feet. She paid for her ticket. Annie is going to try hard. I wish you would give her another chance."

I shook my head. "I can't right now. We can talk tomorrow. What time is her flight?"

"We are taking a cab to the airport at ten in the morning and I'll be picking up our truck from there too."

"Fine, I will be home after then." Before he could say any more, I ended the call.

CHAPTER 28

Sadie was a true friend, and made it easy for me when I asked if I could spend the night. "Of course you can. Make yourself at home," she said, with a huge smile from the embrace of Logan's arms. The love they felt for each other seeped from their eyes. Sadie was right. Eloping was not a mistake. They were meant for each other.

The next morning I thanked Sadie and Logan before they left for work, and a few hours later, Maggie and I headed home, knowing it was safe to return with no risk of running into Annie.

I laughed, as I watched Maggie race through the condo, checking every familiar space, and made herself comfy in her bed, which I had placed in its regular spot by the couch.

There was still a slight smell of smoke throughout the condo, and I went around and opened all the windows. When I entered the spare room, I saw the scorched pillow and headboard. The bed was destroyed. Anger ripped through me as I marched over to the bed and threw the pillow and still damp blanket across the room. I wanted any reminders of Annie out of my home, and stripped the bed, and threw all the bedding in the hallway, until only a bare mattress and bed frame remained. After tossing all the bedding in the trash can outside, I struggled with the mattress, got it to the top of the stairs, then pushed it down and cringed when it took a few photos off the wall with it, that shattered on the stairs. Once it was at the bottom of the stairs, I squeezed by the mattress, pressing my body against the wall, and then dragged it out to the back deck, where I let it fall. Still raged with disgust, and after catching my breath, I marched back upstairs and fought for the next hour with a screwdriver to break down the headboard and frame before taking it outside.

With a few broken nails, and a large scratch on my thigh from a screw sticking out of the headboard, I swore it would be the first and last time I picked up a tool. Satisfied that the last remaining ghosts of Annie were no longer in the house, I checked my phone, and saw there was another text from my mom that simply said, *Please call me. I miss you.* Out of disgust, I threw my phone on the couch. I'd had enough of thinking about her for the day. How could she miss me? She lived halfway across the world. It's not like we saw each other every day. Another pity cry from mom was all it was. I shook off any remaining thoughts and headed for the shower. The smell of smoke lingered in my hair, on my skin, all from removing the bed.

I smiled at my precious girl, Maggie, when I found her lying on the bathroom mat in front of the shower. She sat up when I stepped out and pawed my leg as I stroked the top of her head. "Hey girl." After drying off and dressing in a pair of Levi shorts and a tank top, I gave my hair a quick brush, then headed downstairs with Maggie close behind. Halfway down the stairs, Maggie raced past me, barking and almost knocking me down. "Hey Maggie, slow down. You almost made me break my neck," I yelled. "Why are you so excited? There is no one here." But I was wrong. When I reached the bottom of the stairs, Ricky greeted me holding a dozen pink roses.

He smiled and held out the flowers. "Hey, I'm really sorry. These are for you."

I wasn't too eager to let him off the hook so easily. He had put me through hell this week to save his sister, and I had sacrificed a lot. I took the roses and breathed in their scent. "Thank you. They are beautiful, but I'm still mad."

Ricky rolled his eyes and held out his arms. "Come on, babe. It's just you and me now. Let me make it up to you."

He was blocking the bottom of the stairs, and I gave him a hard stare while smelling the roses again. "So does Annie hate me now?"

Ricky shook his head and took my free hand. "No, she doesn't hate you, but she understands why you hate her. She feels terrible."

I pushed myself past him and headed to the kitchen in search of a vase. Ricky followed.

"And so she should be," I replied, while searching the cabinets. My back facing him. "She almost burnt our house down, Ricky. I have every right to be mad. It was the last straw." I turned to face him, holding a vase. "I couldn't take any more, and then when you started defending her, I was done. There was no way I could agree to her staying here. She would have torn us apart. I mean, look at our honeymoon. It was a disaster."

Ricky inched closer, and slowly took the vase from my hand, and set it on the counter behind me. "I said I was sorry." He leaned in and kissed me gently on the lips. "I love you."

I was losing my battle to stay angry with him, and met his warm lips. The kiss was slow and soft. "Do you still love me?" he whispered.

My eyes were closed, and I didn't want to break away from our kiss, and ignored his question. His tongue found mine, and I could feel my legs weakening when he took me in his arms and pulled me in. I didn't resist, and wrapped my arms around his waist, and pushed my body up against his. This is what I had been yearning for. Me and Ricky, alone with no interruptions. "I do love you, Ricky," I whispered. "And I missed this. I missed us."

We kissed harder, our hands caressing each other's upper bodies, as I leaned back against the pantry door where we had shifted to during our kiss. I had no willpower and gave in to the passion between us. Pressed against the wooden door of the pantry, I rolled Ricky's T-shirt up over his chest and away from his body. "Make love to me," I whispered, as I tossed his shirt across the kitchen, kissing his tight chest. "I want you," I moaned.

Ricky's breathing elevated to pants of passion, as he felt under my tank top and fondled my breasts. "I want you too." Without taking his eyes off me, he pulled away, and with speed, undressed until he stood naked before me. His manhood, ready to satisfy me. I matched his speed, and pulled off my shorts and tank top, kissing him passionately as he took me in his arms and smothered me with his scent. As we kissed hard, and with lust, my arms wrapped around his neck. Ricky took a good hold of my waist and picked me up, all the while, not breaking our kiss. I held on tight with my arms as he braced my body against his, pressing me hard against the pantry door. With my legs wrapped around his waist, Ricky supported my thighs with his powerful hands as we continued to kiss passionately, losing all self-control. My chest heaved when he entered me as he thrust his hips gently so as to be in rhythm. Our bodies began to sweat as our lovemaking increased to short and harder thrusts. My back was sliding down the wooden door of the pantry, and I tightened my grip around Ricky's neck as he continued to ride me to a climax. Our moans became louder, and our breathing changed to heavy pants. Ricky's hands dug into my thighs as he reached orgasm. Within seconds, I joined him, and peaked to a magnificent orgasm.

Sweat beaded on my brow, and my hair was drenched as I stayed in Ricky's grip. My legs were still wrapped around his waist, and my arms were around his neck. My head rested on his shoulder as I tried to catch my breath. "Now that was better than the entire honeymoon," I laughed.

Ricky held me steady as I slowly returned my feet to the floor.

"I love you so much. Let's not fight anymore," I pleaded, before kissing him on the lips.

With his arms still around my waist, he swayed my body gently from side-to-side. "Never again. I'm a basket case when we fight." He pulled away and grabbed his jeans off the floor. "Hey, I should go take care of the spare bedroom. I need to get that bed out of here."

I gave him a cocky smile. "All taken care of. It's outside on the back deck."

Ricky's eyes grew wide with disbelief. "What?" he said with a surprised look, as he walked over to the back door and looked out at the deck. "Oh, my god. You weren't kidding. Why didn't you wait for me?"

"Because it smelled like smoke in here. I opened all the windows and dragged the damn thing outside." I patted his chest playfully. "Now, you have the job of getting rid of it."

Ricky held out his chest. "Easy. I'll throw it in the back of the truck and take it to the city dump."

While I was putting on my shorts, Ricky snuck up behind me and took me in his arms. His fingers traced the sensitive area on my neck before kissing my skin softly. "What are you doing?" he whispered in my ear.

I leaned back in his arms. "Getting dressed."

He kissed my neck again. "Well, you took care of the bed, which means I am a free man. We can make up for lost time on our honeymoon. We have a lot of catching up to do."

I turned around to face him and pressed my nose against his. "What do you have in mind?"

He gave me his sexy smile. "Why don't I take you upstairs and show you?"

CHAPTER 29

Ricky and I stayed in bed for the rest of the day and only left to feed Maggie and grab a bottle of wine and two glasses from the kitchen. We were a happily married couple again, and we're looking forward to spending our lives together. The woes of our honeymoon were soon becoming a distant memory, and so was Annie, until she texted Ricky later that night to let him know she had arrived safely at their mom's.

"I wish your mom all the luck in the world," I said sarcastically, before taking a sip of wine. "I hope she treats her better than she did us and doesn't steal from her."

Ricky leaned back against the pillow. "Come on Jill, let's not start this again. We have spent all afternoon making love and being happy. Don't let a text from my sister ruin it. She's not going to steal from our mom. She is excited about getting her life back on track, and we helped her do that."

"Yeah and it cost us 7,000 dollars and a honeymoon, and let's not forget a bed."

"She'll pay us back. You watch. We talked a lot on the way to the airport. This is just what she needed. Mom is going to help her, and I think she is going to be just fine."

"Well, I'm not holding my breath. I don't want to talk about her anymore. I've been so happy all day with just you. Let's not mention her name again, okay? I want to fall asleep in your arms thinking happy thoughts."

The next morning, Maggie was back to her routine of waking us up by jumping on the bed, followed by a loud bark, to let us know it was time to get up, let her outside and feed her.

After reluctantly pulling myself out of bed and attending to Maggie's needs, I put on a pot of coffee. Ricky soon joined me, shirtless, wearing only a pair of black jeans. He took a seat at the table where I sat scrolling on my phone, raked his hands through his hair, and yawned. "What time is it?"

"A little after nine. You slept in," I said, with a devious smile.

He returned the smile. "It's all your fault. I'm going to give Slater a call in a while, and see when he wants me to come back to work. I can start sooner than next Monday if he needs me, seeing how we are back early."

"Good idea. He could probably use the help." My phone pinged. I saw it was a message from my mom. I released a heavy sigh. "Not again."

Ricky creased his brow. "Who is it?"

"My mom." I read the text to myself and immediately became confused. "What?" I said out loud, with a creased brow.

Concerned about my confusion, Ricky sat up in his chair. "What did she say?"

"Listen to this. It doesn't make any sense." I read the text to him. "Jill, please text me back or call me. We are leaving tomorrow. I would really love to see you before we go. Your father and I miss you, princess." I gave Ricky a puzzled look. "What does she mean she is leaving tomorrow? She already left."

"Maybe she didn't," Ricky replied.

"Well, she didn't come to our wedding, and she checked out of the hotel. She's definitely not here."

Ricky grinned. "Now hold on a second. You assumed she checked out of the hotel, but you don't know for sure. Sounds to me like she didn't."

I picked up my phone and read the message again. "Oh, that's impossible. I know she left. She's just toying with me, to get me to call her. I'm not falling for it. This is how my mom works."

"I think you should call her," Ricky suggested.

I folded my arms and leaned back in my chair. "Why are you siding with her?"

Ricky laughed at my comment. "I'm not siding with anyone, but don't you want to know if she is still here, and how would you feel if you found out later that she was and you missed the opportunity to fix this mess with her?"

"You really think she might still be here?"

Ricky picked up my phone. "Only one way to find out."

I reluctantly took the phone. "Fine, I'll prove to you that you are wrong, and this is just another little game of hers." I located her number and made the call. After a few rings, I heard my mom's voice and put her on speaker.

"Princess, is that you?"

I rolled my eyes. "Yes, mom, it's me. Where are you?"

"We are still at the hotel. We leave tomorrow. I'm so happy you called. Can we see you before we leave?"

I sat up, my eyes bulging. "Wait, you are still at the hotel in San Diego?"

"Yes, I couldn't leave after our horrible misunderstanding. Please princess, your father and I would love to buy you lunch, and Ricky too, if he can join us." I glanced over at Ricky, who was beaming a huge smile at being right. He nodded.

I was unsure what to say. I felt like I was being put on the spot. There was no time to think about what I wanted to do. "Er, yes,

Ricky is here. He said he can join us. I guess we will see you for lunch. What time?"

"Oh, thank you. Is twelve okay? We have an afternoon flight tomorrow, and we need to do a lot of packing."

"Er, yes, that's fine. We will see you then."

Feeling numb, I ended the call and gave Ricky a blank stare. "You were right. She never left."

Ricky smacked his thigh. "I told you."

I shook my head. "Why did I agree to meet with her? I'm only going to leave upset again. I should never have said yes."

"Because you love her, and deep down you know you want to fix this."

I laughed out loud. "You met her. You saw what a witch she is. Let me tell you something. The only way she can fix this is if she gives me an apology. I deserve that much. Don't you agree?"

Ricky gave me a caring smile and took my hand. "I'm not going to argue with that. She owes you an apology. Maybe that is why she wants to see you."

"My mother has never apologized for anything in her life. You may have been right about her still being here, but this you are definitely wrong about."

CHAPTER 30

We arrived at the hotel ten minutes early, but I didn't want to appear anxious, so I asked Ricky if we could wait in the truck for a bit to calm my nerves.

He rubbed my shoulder and gave me a gentle kiss on the cheek. "Sure. Take all the time you need. Everything is going to be okay."

I rubbed my sweaty palms on my jeans. "Why am I so nervous? I hate that she makes me feel this way. She always has."

"Well, now is the time to turn that around. You stood up to her last time. You can do it again, but without the name calling or attitude," Ricky joked.

"I don't know if I can hold back. She brings out the worst in me. There is one thing I am adamant about, though."

Ricky looked concerned. "What's that?"

"If she offers to send us money again, I don't want it. I don't want her having that power over me. Maybe she will treat me with more respect if she sees we are making it on our own."

"That's fine with me. We are both working. We will be okay, and Slater has even hinted at giving me a raise since he has pretty much made me foreman."

A few minutes later, after some more reassuring words from Ricky, I was feeling more confident, and let him know I was ready to face the storm.

"That's my girl," he said with a warm smile.

After exiting the truck Ricky took my hand, and we headed towards the familiar bar where I last saw my mom and dad. I spotted them immediately, sitting next to a window, looking out over the gardens. Mom was dressed in a yellow dress, and dad was wearing his normal Hawaiian shirt attire. They seemed to be in deep conversation, which explained why they hadn't seen us enter. My heart raced as we neared their table, and I took a deep breath to calm my nerves.

"Hello mom," I said, in a flat tone.

Their conversation came to an immediate stop, and both turned their heads to look our way.

My mom was the first to react with a high-pitched squeal, as she stood with open arms, "Princess! You're here!" She moved towards me and pulled me into her space. "Give your mommy a hug."

My body was tense, while my arms remained limp at my sides as I felt my mom's embrace. The powerful scent of her perfume caused me to turn my head away, which my mom mistook as an invitation for her to kiss my cheek. I didn't return the hug or kiss, and took a seat next to my dad, across from my mom. My dad gave me a nod. "How are you doing, princess?"

"Okay, and you, dad?"

"As good as can be. Your mother has missed you, though."

Ricky took a seat next to me and across from my dad. I immediately took his hand and crossed my legs, thankful that I had dressed casually in jeans and a crisp white shirt. It was important for me to not get dressed up like my mother would have expected, and just allow myself to be me.

For a few seconds, there was an uncomfortable silence, while my parents took some large sips from their glasses of wine. Their nerves were showing. I leaned back in my chair while Ricky ordered us drinks from the waiter that approached our table. Seeing my parent's nervous disposition upon our arrival was something I wasn't used to. To my surprise, it put my own nerves at ease. For the first time, I felt in control and confident I could handle anything my mom threw at me.

My mom narrowed her eyes as she gave me the once over. "What are you wearing?"

I immediately stood and let out a loud grunt. I wasn't going to be intimidated by her anymore. "That's it, I'm leaving. You can't resist attacking me, can you, Mom?"

My mother's jaw dropped. "I only asked what you were wearing. I'm not used to seeing you dress so casually. Especially in jeans."

I snarled when I spoke. "It's your tone, mom. It's so degrading. I happen to like jeans. They are comfortable and I don't feel like a snob when I wear them."

Ricky took my hand. "Calm down, Jill, sit down." He released a heavy sigh. "Let's start over."

Ricky tugged at my hand, and I fell back into my chair. I glared at my mom. "I can't believe you are still here. What have you been doing with yourself? By the way, the wedding was beautiful. Too bad you missed it," I said, with a hint of sarcasm.

My mom took my dad's hands. I rarely saw affection between them, so this caught my attention. She looked at my dad before she spoke. "We didn't miss it, princess. We were there. You looked beautiful in your pink dress."

A lump wedged in my throat that I couldn't dislodge, and I squeezed Ricky's hand tighter. "What? You were at our wedding?"

"Yes, we were. You think I would miss my only daughter's wedding? Come on princess, I'll admit, I've done some unforgivable things in my life, but I wouldn't stoop so low as to miss your wedding."

I didn't believe her, but she knew the color of my dress. "I never saw you there. There weren't that many people on the beach."

"We weren't on the beach. We watched from the cliffs above at the end of the parking lot. I cried the entire time. I wanted to tell you so badly how beautiful you looked, and that I loved you. It took all my willpower not to run down to the beach and be by your side. "

I had never seen my mom so emotional. I had no idea what to say. "Then why didn't you, why didn't you come down to the beach?"

"I was afraid to. The way you left, the last time we saw you, I thought you would lash out at us and tell us to leave. I wouldn't have been able to handle that. It would have destroyed me and ruined your wedding."

I tried to defend myself. "Mom, I stormed off because of the way you were talking to me in front of my fiancée and friends. I was embarrassed, and I had every right to be. You did nothing but belittle me and find fault with everything about me. It's something you've done my entire life and I'm just tired of it. Why can't you accept me for who I am and stop trying to turn me into someone like you? I'm not you, and I never will be." My head shook in disbelief. "I can't believe you were at the wedding and we never saw you. Were you at the reception, too?"

"No, we left when we saw the ceremony was over. I just wanted to see my little girl get married." She took a deep breath. "I realize now why you left so abruptly. You pointed out a lot of things about myself that I never saw, and as much as I hate to admit it, you were right. Even your father agrees. He had a few words with me after you left."

I turned and looked at my dad. "You stood up to mom? That's a first."

"Well, after what you said, I guess you opened my eyes, too. I never noticed the way your mom treated you until you pointed it out, and she needed to see it, too. I figured if I said something, she might just pay attention." He smiled at my mom. "Looks like she did."

Ricky surprised me by speaking next. "Can I just say something? I love your daughter with all my heart. She is a beautiful woman, inside and out. When I first met her, she was going through a lot. We met at the hospital where a mutual friend of ours was in a coma after a horrific accident. We didn't know whether he was going to make it. It was during that time that Jill questioned her own life, and what was important to her. That is the Jill I fell in love with. Someone who finally knows herself and doesn't have to prove anything to anyone. Your daughter really is an amazing person. You should be really proud of her. I know I am."

I leaned into Ricky's embrace as he cupped his arm over my shoulder. "Thank you. I love you so much."

"I am proud of my princess," my mother replied, with tears pooling in her eyes. And then she said the words I was waiting to hear. "I'm sorry. I've always just wanted the best for you, and never realized how much I was pushing you away."

I was numb. My mom actually apologized to me. "Yes, you have been pushing me away—to the point where I've been afraid to share anything about me or my life with you, because you would always find a way to find fault with it. And another thing, can you please stop calling me princess? My name is Jill."

"But I've always called you princess, because that is who you are. You are my princess."

"It was fine when I was seven or eight years old, mom, but not now. Please call me Jill. I love my name." I turned and looked at my dad. "And that goes for you, too."

My mother placed her hands in her lap. "Okay, if that is what you wish, I will start calling you Jill."

"Thank you." My mind went back to the wedding. "So after the ceremony, you left? You never went to the reception?"

My mom shook her head. "No, I was too upset. We left and went for a long drive. It took your father hours to console me. I should have been there, and your father should have given you away."

"Mom, you are doing it again. You are playing the guilt card. I was upset, too, that you weren't there, and that dad didn't give me away, but it's because of your controlling ways that led up to us fighting. Don't you get that? And you are still trying to make me feel guilty again by reminding me that dad didn't give me away."

My mom raised her voice a notch. "I'm sorry, okay. I don't realize I'm doing it. It's going to take some time for me to adjust. I don't know what you want from me."

"I want you to just be a mom. Be happy for me when I tell you I am happy. Don't criticize everything I do or tell me your way is better. It may work for you, but not for me. Let me live my life as Jill, your daughter. One that you can be proud of. I want to be able to call you on the phone and share with you what is going on in my life, where you just listen and not judge me."

"I can do that. I can do all of that," my mom said eagerly.

"Can you, mom? Can you just be a mom and not criticize everything I do? If you can't, then there is no hope for us. I'm more confident in myself, and I now know I can stand up to you, and I will."

"I'll make sure she does," my dad announced. "I'll keep her in her place. But I think your mom realizes now that you are your own person, and she needs to stop lecturing you like you are still a young girl. Right, Pauline?"

"Yes, you are all correct. I'm sorry Princess, oops, I mean Jill. I will try to be a better mother. Will you forgive me?"

Listening to my mom gave me goosebumps. Her words and apology were genuine. I felt it. For the first time, she was the one trying to save our relationship. Finally, I think I had gotten through to her. It was up to me to accept her apology so we could move forward with what I hoped to be a true mother and daughter relationship. Silence fell around the table again, as Ricky and my parents waited with anticipation for me to speak. I squeezed Ricky's hand as I spoke and looked directly at my mom.

"I accept your apology mom, and I also owe you an apology for embarrassing you in front of my friends. Two wrongs do not make a right, and even though we both agree you were disrespectful to me in front of my friends and Ricky, I was also disrespectful to you, so I am sorry, too."

My mom released a huge sigh of relief. "Oh, thank you. Can I have a hug?"

I gave her a smile before leaving my seat and walking to her side of the table. "Yes, you can have a hug."

After the initial *make up* hug, and after I had returned to my seat, my mom slid an envelope across the table.

I picked it up. "What's this?" I asked, with a creased brow.

"It's your wedding present. If you haven't gone on your honeymoon yet, you can use it for that."

"We just got back from our honeymoon."

"Well, that was fast," my mom said. "Where did you go?"

"We went to Las Vegas. Someday I will tell you about it, just not now." I opened the envelope and saw it was a check in the amount of $10,000.

"Mom, dad, you didn't have to do this. That's a lot of money. Besides, I thought you said you weren't going to give me any more money now that I'm married."

My dad spoke. "Well, that's true, but this is a wedding present. It's different. But I would like to say, if you still need us to send you money, we will continue to do so. Your mother told me what she had said about not sending you any more money. It was said in the heat of the moment. I reminded her that you two are just starting out. You may need help."

I gave my dad a smile. "Thanks, Dad, but Ricky and I have already talked about this, and we are going to be just fine. We will put this money away for a rainy day. If I'm going to live my life the way I want to live it, then I need to be independent."

My dad took my hand and gave it a light kiss. "I understand. I have to say, you looked beautiful on your wedding day. Even I shed a tear or two. You made me very proud, even though you didn't know we were there. Sorry we missed the reception, by the way. How was it?"

I patted the back of my dad's hand. "It was probably a good thing you didn't go. A man was killed, and Slater ended up in the hospital with a gunshot wound."

My mother raised her hand to her chest and shrieked. "Oh, my goodness! What in heaven's name happened?"

I gave my mom a brief rundown of the reception. "It was terrifying. Davin was the one that got killed. He used to date Sabela, and showed up at the wedding with a gun and shot Slater, but not before Slater stabbed him with the cake knife. We were lucky it wasn't any worse. If Slater hadn't killed him, who knows what may have happened? He could have killed more."

"And how is Slater?" my dad asked.

"He's okay. It was a flesh wound. He is home now."

My mom expressed her relief. "Thank god for that."

We continued to discuss the events of the wedding reception over lunch without my mom criticizing me or judging me. My parents got to know Ricky better, and I sensed by the end of lunch they had grown quite fond of him. He made them laugh, and expressed his love for me many times.

We left on good terms, and I felt my relationship with my parents had made a sharp turn. It was a positive move that looked promising. My mom was finally seeing her daughter as a woman and not a little girl. The future looked good for the two of us. I think we have finally broken the barrier between my mom and I.

CHAPTER 31

"I'm so proud of you," Ricky said, on the way home in the truck. "I wasn't sure at first because you said you wanted to leave a few minutes after we got there. But you soon calmed down and held it together."

I chuckled. "I didn't know if I could, but my mood shifted when my mom started being truthful with me and actually showing some emotions. My whole life I thought she was made of cardboard," I joked. "I've never seen her shed a tear or show any feelings. When she did, it changed my entire perspective of her. For the first time, I saw her not just as a mom, but as a human being. It was quite an eye opener." I gave him a warm smile. "I feel good about everything. If she keeps this up, I won't be embarrassed to call her my mom."

"Well, I think you are off to a good start. She said she would call you once they arrived in Spain. I have a sense it's going to be a good phone call. Much better than the previous ones."

I smiled again, before resting my head on his shoulder. "Yeah, I'm actually looking forward to it."

After stopping off at the bank to deposit the check from my parents into the savings account, we spent the afternoon shopping for a new bed for the spare bedroom. After searching in three stores, we eventually found one that we both agreed on. It had a wooden, white-washed headboard and footboard, and because we were driving the truck, we were able to take it home that day.

I tried my best trying to help Ricky put it together, but I felt I was more in the way than helping him. I didn't have the strength to hold the heavy headboard up as he tried to screw it to the frame, and dropped it many times. Once on his hand.

"How did you ever manage to take the old bed apart?" he laughed. "You are hopeless at this stuff."

I shrugged my shoulders while struggling to hold the headboard up for the fourth time. "It was easy to take it apart. It didn't take much thinking, and I pretty much just pushed everything down the stairs. I'm surprised I only broke two picture frames. And to think, Sabela did construction with Slater every day when she first met him. I don't know how she did it?"

"She loved it and she was good at it. Slater would only have to show her how to do something once, and she would catch on immediately. She had a knack for it. I don't think you do," he said, with a loud laugh.

I felt myself losing my grip on the headboard again. My hands were sliding. "Are you almost done? I'm about to drop it. Hurry up."

Ricky worked the electric drill harder. "Hold on. Almost there." With one last squeeze of the trigger, he screwed the screw in at a faster pace. "There we go. All done. Only about twenty more screws to go."

I rolled my eyes. "Come on, let's get this done. My back is killing me and I need to feed Maggie."

An hour later, the bed was complete, and I left the room hastily before Ricky had the chance to corner me on another home project. I had a new feeling of admiration for Sabela, not understanding why she enjoyed working in construction.

After Maggie was fed and Ricky had finished in the spare bedroom, we settled on the couch to watch a movie. I was enjoying our quality time together before going back to work next week. We were definitely making up for time lost on our honeymoon, and I was soaking it all up.

My phone rang the minute we got comfortable on the couch, with Maggie snuggled up to my thigh next to me. I released a heavy sigh and grabbed it from the coffee table. It was Claire.

Ricky paused the movie, and I answered the call. "Hey Claire."

"Jill. I just got off the phone with Sabela, and she said you were home already. What happened? She mentioned something about you having a fall out with Ricky's sister. She said that you bumped into her in Vegas. Is that right?"

"Yeah, something like that. It's a long story, but she ended up ruining our honeymoon. We are having more fun spending time together at home than in Vegas. We should have just stayed home," I laughed.

"I'm sorry to hear that. Is his sister still in Vegas, or is she living there now?"

I didn't want to get into the whole story. Eventually it will come out and I gave her some short answers to satisfy her. "She was living in Vegas, but now living with her mom. Ricky arranged it all."

"Oh, good for Ricky. I hope everything works out for her."

"Yeah, me too," I said in a flat tone, still not having a care in the world about what happened to her. I quickly changed the subject to prevent my mood from changing. "So what's up? How is married life for you and Travis?"

"We are doing great, and Travis' mom is still with us. I'm so glad we found her. I haven't regretted it for one second. You've been there since the beginning. I can't thank you enough. Everything worked out. They get along really well."

"Oh, I'm so happy to hear that. It was a tearjerker at the

wedding, to see them meet for the first time. When does she go home?"

"Next week. In fact, it's why I'm calling you. When I heard you guys were home, I thought it would be nice if we all got together for dinner before she leaves, so you can meet her and spend some time with her. I can guarantee you will love her like we do. I see a lot of Travis in her. They have the same smile, and their eyes are the same color, too."

"We would love to. What a great idea! Would it be at your place?"

"I was thinking about having it at Slater and Sabela's. Their place is bigger, including her kitchen, but I have to run it by her first. We are going over there tomorrow to discuss the children's home, so I will bring it up."

"Oh, how is that going?" I asked.

"It's going well. Quicker than we expected. We are really excited about it, and I may have some more news over dinner."

I was intrigued. "Really? Like what?"

"I can't say yet until we have our meeting tomorrow."

I laughed. "Well, you can't keep me hanging. That's mean."

Ricky gave me a puzzled look. "What are you talking about?" he whispered.

"The children's home," I whispered back, before returning to speak to Claire. "Well, I can't wait to see you and find out what news you have. Call me after you've talked to Sabela."

"I will, bye."

After ending the call, I leaned back against the couch.

Ricky gave me a concerned look? "Is everything okay?"

"Yeah, I think so. Claire wants us all to have dinner together before Travis's mom goes home. But she also said she may have some news." I creased my brow as I looked at Ricky. "What do you think that could be? She can't be pregnant. She can't have kids."

Ricky shrugged his shoulders. "Don't try to guess. You are never right," he laughed. "I'm sure she will tell us when she is ready."

"Oh, but I hate the waiting game."

CHAPTER 32

Claire called me back the next day while Ricky and I were giving Maggie a bath outside. Covered in soapsuds, I moaned at Claire's bad timing. Ricky took the leash and struggled on his own to keep Maggie in place, who stood in a kiddie pool dripping wet and covered in soap. "Can you manage?" I asked, as I stepped away and wiped my hands on my jeans before reaching for my phone on the patio table.

Ricky nodded, while keeping a firm hold on Maggie. "I'll do my best."

I took a seat and answered the call. "Hey, Claire."

"Hey, Jill. Are you guys free tomorrow for dinner?"

The urgency in her voice took me aback. "Tomorrow? What's the rush?"

"We have some exciting news. I can't wait to share it with you. Please say you will come."

"Yes, of course. Are you at least going to give me a hint?" Suddenly my eyes grew wide, and I let out a loud scream, as I saw Maggie race towards me, soaking wet. "No, Maggie!" I yelled, followed by a roaring laugh, as she stood next to me and shook her thick fur coat many times. "Oh my god, Maggie. I'm soaked." I laughed some more, with echoes of Ricky laughing by the pool.

"I couldn't hold on to her," he laughed.

I wiped the excess water from my jeans and shook my hands as Maggie was satisfied with her shaking techniques, and trotted back over to Ricky, who dried her off with a towel. "Little late for the towel," I hollered, and then remembered Claire was still on the line. I wiped the beads of water off the screen. "Claire, are you still there?"

"Yes, I'm here. What's going on?" she laughed. "Are you having a party?"

"Yes, a pool party. We were trying to give Maggie a bath, and she escaped from Ricky and shook right in front of me. I'm drenched."

"Oh, I'm glad my Tilly is a small dog and doesn't have much fur. I'm excited that you can make it tomorrow. Does six work for you?"

"Yes, we will bring some wine. Is there anything else you want us to bring?"

"No, this is on me and Travis. I told Sabela the same thing. She has her hands full with the twins and Scottie. We are bringing everything."

"Great, we can't wait. Hey, would you mind if I invite Logan and Sadie? They were at our wedding, and she found us the great wedding dress store where we bought our dresses. I would love for them to hang out with us more. Sadie has been a good friend. She was there for me when Travis and I broke up, and watched Maggie when we went to Vegas."

"I think that's a great idea. Yes, please do."

"Thanks, I'll call them." I paused for a moment, unsure of my next question. "Hey Claire, how are you doing since the reception? Davin was your brother. I'm sure this has to be hard for you."

There was silence. "Claire?"

Her tone was flat. "I don't want to talk about it right now."

"I understand. I'm sorry for bringing it up." I quickly changed the subject. "Okay, I'm going to give Ricky a hand with Maggie. We will see you tomorrow."

After ending the call, Ricky seemed to have Maggie under control and was now playing catch with her. I leaned back in my chair and admired the view before me. I laughed when Maggie ran into him and knocked him to the ground, where they wrestled. Maggie barked with joy, and Ricky laughed as Maggie pinned him to the ground to smother his face with puppy kisses.

While watching the heartwarming scene, I found myself for the first time thinking of kids. I was picturing Ricky playing with our child instead of Maggie, and it gave me goosebumps. Having children had never crossed my mind. This time last year, I was single and envious of all my friends, because they had all found their true loves and were settling down. Now, here I am, a year later, married to the best guy ever, imagining we have a child. The idea of me being a mother seemed so foreign, but then again, I never thought of Sabela being one, and she fits the role perfectly. She's a great mom to Scottie and the twins.

I tried to shake the crazy thoughts I was having, but I couldn't. The idea of having Ricky's baby was growing on me the more I watched Ricky and Maggie play. I couldn't help but think what a great dad he would be. Ricky and I had always had the plan to enjoy each other for a while before discussing the huge step of having a child. Ricky is a few years younger than me, and I'm sure he has never had such thoughts as what I was experiencing now. I laughed out loud when Ricky fell to the ground again, knocked over by Maggie.

"Do you want to come join us?" he yelled. "Maggie is strong. I need some help," he joked.

I laughed again as I stood and ran over to Ricky, now pinned to the ground again by Maggie. To save him, I retrieved the ball laying next to his head. "Hey Maggie, come on, fetch the ball," I hollered, as I threw it away from Ricky. Maggie immediately raced to where the ball had landed, allowing Ricky to brush off his clothes and stand up.

He wrapped his arms around my waist and smiled. "I sure do love you."

I leaned into his space and kissed him tenderly on the lips. "I love you, too, and was enjoying watching you and Maggie wrestle, but was having some really weird thoughts."

Ricky creased his brow. "Like what?"

I released a nervous laugh. "I was picturing you playing with our kid, just like you were playing with Maggie. It gave me goosebumps."

His reaction disappointed me. I knew I was testing him to see if he had ever had any similar thoughts. He chuckled and shook his head. "Oh, my goodness. You have been out in the sun too long. You are hallucinating. Us, with kids? Can you even imagine?" He wrapped his arms around my shoulder, and I buried my head in his chest so he wouldn't see the disappointment on my face. "Now that is funny, Jill. Come on, let's go inside. Maggie is dry enough now."

CHAPTER 33

The subject of children never came up again for the rest of the night. Ricky had made it clear he wasn't thinking of having children anytime soon, and maybe I was just caught up in the moment by letting my thoughts spill over to Sabela and her kids.

I called Sadie and invited her to the dinner party tomorrow night. "We would love to," she squealed into the phone. "I haven't seen any of you guys, except for you, since the wedding. What should I bring?"

"Just yourselves. This is Claire's treat."

Sadie protested. "Oh no, I must bring something. How about some wine?"

"Nope. Me and Ricky are bringing some."

"Okay then, I will bring some beer."

"Sounds good. We will see you tomorrow. I will text you Sabela's address."

Later that night, my mom called me to let me know they had arrived home in Spain. We talked for almost an hour. I think it may have been our longest call ever. For the first time, I had no anxieties while speaking to her, or afraid of saying the wrong thing. She was pleasant, and even complimented me a few times and told me how much she liked Ricky. When she told me she missed me, I told her I missed her too, and I meant it. We had turned over a new leaf into our relationship, and I saw only good things ahead.

I smiled and cuddled close to Ricky, who sat next to me, dressed in only a pair of boxers. He smelt fresh from his recent shower and I kissed his chest. "Hmm, you smell good."

He leaned in closer and kissed me passionately on the lips while reaching inside my silk pink bathrobe to fondle my breast. "And so do you." He looked into my eyes and smiled. "You're happy, aren't you?"

I smiled back. "I am. It felt good to have a decent conversation with my mom. Even my dad got on the phone and seemed much happier. I guess mom is more pleasant to be around," I joked.

Ricky kissed me again. "That's all I want is for you to be happy. When you're happy, I'm happy."

"You make me happy, Ricky. These few days at home with you have been amazing. I feel so close to you." I rubbed his chest. His skin was firm and tanned, with very few chest hairs. I closed my eyes when he pulled me in closer and kissed me with more passion than before.

"You are the woman for me, Jill," he whispered, before sliding my bathrobe down past my shoulders and kissing my bare skin. I melted beneath his touch and leaned back against the couch, yearning for him to take me. Using his tongue, he gently followed my neckline down to the V in my bathrobe. I released a soft moan as he reached inside my robe and pulled it open. I aided him by untying the belt and spreading it open.

Ricky took in a deep breath as he admired my naked body before him. "You are magnificent. How did I ever get so lucky?" he said, before burying his head in my chest.

I moaned again and arched my back. "The same way I got to be lucky," I whispered, as he kissed my naked skin and teased me with his tongue. Within minutes, he, too, was naked. And I laid down on the couch, my legs wrapped around his waist so he could enter me. The love making was soft and gentle. We kissed with passion, and whispered our love for each other, as we caressed each other's body with butterfly kisses and soothing strokes. It was long and passionate. This was more than making love. This was a deep connection that I had not felt before, and it felt so right. We had become one. With Ricky, I was home.

CHAPTER 34

The following night, Ricky and I were the last to arrive at Sabela's for dinner. It was the first time I had seen everyone in the same room since the wedding. It was a warm evening with a gentle breeze, and the door was wide open. We entered without knocking, and were greeted by smiling faces and friendly waves. It felt good to be amongst my friends again.

Claire and Sabela were sitting on the couch with the twins. Logan and Sadie were standing in the kitchen talking to Slater, Travis, and Travis's mom, Caroline, who stood by the stove stirring something in a pot. I noticed Scottie tugging on Slater's arm for attention while his dad was in a deep conversation, and it made me smile.

Slater met us at the door, and took the bottles of wine that Ricky was carrying. After a friendly handshake and a pat on the shoulder, Slater turned to me and gave me a hug.

"Hey, guys. It's so good to see you. Come on in, I'll grab you a drink."

Ricky held me in his arms as we spoke to Slater. "You're looking good, Slater. You heal quickly," Ricky said.

"Thanks, man. My side is still a little sore. But other than that, I'm doing great. Still no heavy lifting, though. So whenever you want to come back to work, you can. No need to wait till Monday."

"Me and Jill were just talking about that. I can be there tomorrow," Ricky told him.

Slater smiled. "Fantastic. I'll text you the address of where we are working."

Claire left the couch, and on her way to the kitchen, stopped to say hi to us.

I gave her a warm smile. "Hey Claire, do you need any help?"

She shook her head. "Nope. I have it all under control. It's easy, and Travis' mom is an enormous help. We are having spaghetti, garlic bread, and a salad. It should be ready in about half an hour. I'm just going to go check on the sauce."

"So, when are you going to share the exciting news?" I asked.

She gave me a big smile. "Over dinner."

"Well, let's hurry up and eat," I joked, before heading over to Sabela, who was sitting on the couch. A few minutes later, we were joined by Sadie, while Logan continued to talk to Travis.

I took a seat next to Sabela and looked at one of the twins cradled in her arms. The other slept in the bassinet next to her. "How are my baby girls?" I whispered.

Sabela whispered back. "They are good and growing so fast. They just ate. Hope fell asleep in my arms and I'm afraid to move. I may wake her up."

I gazed at Hope's precious face. She had grown in the short time we had been gone. Her rosy cheeks seemed fuller, and her eyelashes longer. My heart was full. "She is beautiful, just like her mama."

"They bring us such happiness," Sabela said, with a warm smile. "And Scottie has taken well to being the big brother. He is so protective of them. You should see them together," she chuckled. "He is so gentle." She released a small laugh. "Just the other day, I laid Joy on the couch to change her diaper, and Scottie raced upstairs and came back down with two pillows, placing them on the floor in front of the couch in case she rolled off."

I glanced over at Joy, still sleeping soundly in the bassinet. "Aww, that is so sweet. He will always be their protector."

Sadie knelt beside the bassinet and stroked Joy's delicate hand.

"She is so tiny. How do you have time to do anything, Sabela? I don't know how you do it."

"Slater is a lot of help. I'd be a basket case if I had to do all this on my own. He lets me sleep most of the night, then feeds the girls when they wake up. He's a wonderful dad."

"They have his nose," I commented. "I wonder what their hair will be like?"

"Slater had curly, dark brown hair when he was a kid, and you can see Scottie has the same. It will be some time before these two start growing any good amount of hair."

I couldn't help but notice Sadie's dreamy eyes as she continued to look at Joy and smile. "Do you and Logan plan on having any kids?" I asked.

Sadie looked up. "We've talked about it. But I think I'm more keen than him. He wants to someday," she giggled. "But don't tell him. I'm ready now. We are not getting any younger. I don't want to be an old lady when my kids are in their teens."

"Well, then you should tell him," Sabela announced. "The girls were not planned, but they are the best thing that happened to us."

"Yeah, you really should let Logan know how you feel," I added.

Sadie smiled. "What about you and Ricky? Any kids in your near future?"

I thought of my admission to Ricky yesterday when he was bathing Maggie, and my heart sank. I shook my head. "No, we don't have any plans."

Sabela tapped my knee with her free hand. "Well, don't leave it too long. Like Sadie said, we are not getting any younger."

I quickly stood up. "Hey, I'm going to go say hi to Travis and his mom."

I noticed the quick glance Sabela and Sadie gave each other when I made my sudden departure. I knew they'd sensed my mood change, and was relieved they didn't question it.

Sabela simply nodded. "Okay."

Travis and his mom, Caroline, were now sitting at the table with Slater and Ricky, playing cards. They all looked up and smiled when Ricky pulled out a chair for me. "Have a seat. We are playing a mean hand of poker for Cheerios," Ricky said, before giving me a peck on the cheek.

I laughed when I saw the pile of cereal in front of everyone, and a larger pile in the middle of the table. "Now this is how they should do it in Vegas. It would be a lot cheaper," I joked, as I leaned into Ricky and checked out his hand.

"How's your week been with your mom?" I asked Travis.

Travis gave his mom a loving smile. "It's been amazing. I now know where I get some of my bad habits," he joked.

His mom slapped his shoulder. "It's been wonderful. There were so many unanswered questions that have been answered. We have spent so many late nights talking and getting to know each other, and looking at photos."

It was beautiful to see them together. "I can see the resemblance. You have your mom's good looks, Travis."

I joined in on the next game and screamed out loud when Ricky won my entire pile of cereal. Ricky leaned in and gave me a quick kiss on the lips before standing. "I'm done. I have a life's supply of Cheerios now. Scottie and I are going to play some video games before dinner."

I remained in the kitchen to help the others set the table and serve the food.

Sabela managed to lay Hope in the other bassinet without waking her up, and joined all of us at the table, while Claire and Travis's mom placed the food in the center.

Slater was the first to grab a plate. "It smells and looks great, Claire." He nudged Scottie's shoulder with his, who sat next to him. "Want me to fix you a plate, buddy?"

Scottie nodded. "Yes, please, and I want lots of sauce."

Over dinner, we were asked questions about our honeymoon from hell, and Ricky and I filled them in on all the details. The girls sided with my anger, and agreed that I had every right to be upset and not trust her, but Slater, as always, showed me another side.

"It's a shame she ruined your honeymoon, Jill, but to me, it sounds like it was a blessing in disguise. I'd hate to think where she would be a year from now if you two hadn't gotten her out of there."

I disagreed. "But she stole a lot of money from us. How can I ever forgive her for that?"

Slater leaned back in his chair and chuckled, which irked me. "It's just money, Jill. We are talking about a life here. A life that was lost and needed to be rescued. She was obviously desperate. Don't give up on her. She may surprise you and pay you back. After all, she told you she would."

"I'm not holding my breath."

Slater continued to defend Annie. "Put yourself in her shoes. What would you do if you came across that much money and knew it could change your life?"

I snapped back. "I would never do what she did, especially to my family."

Slater shrugged his shoulders. "In desperate times, we do desperate things. Never say never. You are going to have to show some forgiveness to Annie sooner or later. She is Ricky's sister. You can't expect him to disown her because of how you feel."

I glanced around the table and saw the women were all giving slight nods, agreeing with Slater. It seemed I had lost their support.

I rolled my eyes. "I'm done talking about this. My good mood is slipping." I turned and faced Claire. "You said you had an announcement. Let's hear it. I need some good news."

Everyone around the table shifted their focus to Claire and echoed, "Yes, Claire. We are waiting."

Claire took Travis's hand. "Do you want to tell them?"

ravis shifted in his seat and took a swig of beer.

"Come on, guys. Don't keep us waiting. We are dying to hear what you have to tell us," Ricky hollered.

Claire raised her hands. "Okay, I guess it's time to tell you," she said, while giving Travis's hand an extra hard squeeze.

Travis spoke next. "As you all know, we have been working really hard with Slater and Sabela on the Children's home and adoption agency. I have to tell you, it's not been easy. It has taken hours and hours of frustrating phone calls, and mounds of paperwork to get to where we are today. But Claire and I know it's going to be well worth it." He glanced over at Sabela and Slater and smiled. "I can't thank you guys enough for giving us this chance, and neither can the children that we will be giving a second chance in life and a loving home."

Slater raised his beer. "I couldn't think of a better couple. Now go on, tell them."

"Tell us what?" I asked, while glancing back and forth between Claire, Travis, and Slater.

Claire's eyes sparkled when she spoke. "In two weeks, we will be expecting our first child. It's much sooner than we expected, but we are now official, and we move into the house this weekend." She looked at Travis again. "And we, including Slater and Sabela, have decided on a name for the home. It will be called *Open Arms Children's Home and Adoption Agency*."

Sadie and I gasped at the same time. "Oh, my god! It's really happening," I squealed. "I love that name. It's perfect."

Tears pooled in Claire's eyes. "Yes, it is. We can't believe it. We are going to welcome children into our home and give them a new start in life. Our dream is finally coming true."

"And that's not all," Sabela said, as she pulled Scottie in and kissed the top of his head.

"There's more?" I asked.

"Oh, there is a lot more," Claire said, while looking at Sabela. "Tell them, Sabela."

"Well, we are going to use the adoption agency to allow me to legally adopt Scottie and be his legal mom."

I raised my hand to my mouth. "Oh, that is wonderful. I'm so happy for you."

Slater joined in on the conversation. "I think we should have a moving day and end it with a barbecue at what will be Travis and Claire's new home. We can all help them move and celebrate at the end of the day. What do you say? Who's in?"

I was the first to raise my hand in an excited frenzy. "Me! What fun! You can count me and Ricky in."

Sabela turned and smiled at Slater. "What a brilliant idea. Yes, we will be there, and I'll call my mom. She can come along and watch the twins. I'm sure Scottie would love to help, too." She turned and looked at Scottie. "Right Scottie?"

"You betcha. I'm strong," he boasted, flexing his arms.

Sadie and Logan sat at the end of the table, arm in arm. "We would love to help, too," Logan announced. "I'll close the store early."

Travis took Claire's hand and gave it a hard squeeze. "You guys are amazing. Thank you so much. At least let us feed you and provide the drinks."

Slater raised his glass. "Let's make it a potluck. You put on this fantastic dinner tonight. We will all bring something."

Everyone at the table nodded and agreed, while Sabela went on a hunt for a notepad and pen to write down each of our contributions.

"You know, we still have some more news," Claire announced, while Sabela finished up her list.

The surprised look on Sabela's and Slater's faces told me they weren't expecting any more announcements. "You do?" Slater asked.

Travis looked at his mother with a caring smile before he spoke. "Claire and I had a long chat with my mom, and we have been dreading her leaving. We've missed out on so much. Just when we were finally getting to know each other, it's time for her to leave. Turns out my mom had the same feelings. So Claire and I made her a proposition, and she accepted."

"Well, what is it?" I said impatiently.

Travis took a deep breath. "My mom is going to be the live-in nurse at the home. She will be living with us."

Sabela's eyes grew wide. "What a brilliant idea." She turned and looked at Caroline. "I'm so happy for you. It's perfect. You and Travis will be working together."

Caroline smiled with tears in her eyes. "Thank you. I was not looking forward to returning to my lonely life. I already gave notice at my job, and when Travis and Claire return from their honeymoon, Travis is going to go with me to Seattle to help me move. While they are gone, I will stay at their place with Tilly. They thought it would be best if she stayed with me."

I raised my hands. "Wait. You are going on your honeymoon? I thought you were going to wait until next spring."

Claire laughed. "Well, that was the plan, but everything's happening so fast with the home that once it's open, who knows when we will be able to go, so we've decided we will go next week after the big move."

"Next week!" I squealed. "Wow. So much is going on. My head is spinning."

"Where are you going?" Sabela asked.

"We are going to bootleg it around Yosemite. It's too late to book a campsite. You have to book months in advance, but we like the idea of hiking through the forest and setting up camp along the way."

I leaned back in my chair and shook my head. "Wait, you don't even know where you will sleep? You're just going to pack your stuff and camp wherever you feel like for an entire week? What about showers and a bathroom?"

Travis laughed at my discomfort. "It's called an adventure, Jill. That's what makes it fun. Totally spontaneous and living off the grid with nature. As for showers and bathrooms, streams come in handy for that, and we will be going into Yosemite Park some days to use their amenities."

I shook my head again, not believing what I was hearing. "But there are bears and stuff in the woods. What if one comes inside your tent? You wouldn't catch me doing that."

This time, Claire and Travis echoed their laughs. "We will be fine. We have both camped many times before, and know how to take care of ourselves," Claire said, with another laugh. "You should try it sometime. We want you and Ricky to come camping with us someday. You never know, you might enjoy it."

I shook my head vigorously. "Not on your life," I protested. "Too many bugs, and I like my warm bed. You guys go have fun and you can tell us all about it when you get home. I just hope your honeymoon is better than ours was," I joked.

Everyone smiled at the table as they embraced their loved ones. Slater looked over at Travis and Claire. "And when you both get back, we will all be here to help launch the children's home, *Open Arms.*"

Award winning author, Tina Hogan Grant loves to write stories with strong female characters that know what they want and aren't afraid to chase their dreams. She loves to write sexy and sometimes steamy romances with happy ever after endings.

She is living life to the fullest in a small mountain community in Southern California with her husband and two dogs. When she is not writing she is probably riding her ATV, kayaking or hiking with her best friend – her husband of twenty-five years.

www.tinahogangrant.com

www.ingramcontent.com/pod-product-compliance
Lightning Source LLC
Chambersburg PA
CBHW030754200726
48288CB00004B/1166